Bridal Faire

Realms of Glister Book Two

Melisse Aires

Copyright

This is a work of fiction. Similarities to real people, places, or events are entirely coincidental.
Copyright © 2019 Melisse Aires.
Please leave a review if you enjoyed this book.

Table of Contents

Acknowledgments

Editor: Dave Ellis
Cover: Melisse Aires
Canstock Photos

Newsletter!

Join my newsletter for new release and sales news!
https://sendfox.com/melisseaires

Chapter One

Adler dared not look up from his position when Master Shoji called his name. "Mixing teleth potion," he called. His entire attention focused on the small cauldron over the fire.

One, two, three. The perfume of El flowers filled the room and sparkles of Glister danced above the cauldron.

"Ah, good job, my boy." Master Shoji came into the room since the explosive dangers ended when the sweet scent wafted from the kettle. He wiggled his stubby fingers in the Glister still whirling above the brew. "Perfect! I can tell it will be of outstanding quality. Very helpful next winter when we all catch colds. But I popped in for another reason. Come to me in the garden when you have finished your potion. You have received two wind missives, one from your father and one from your mother."

Master Shoji, even with antlers, only came to Adler's shoulder, but he reached up and patted Adler's arm for comfort. Adler's father often threatened to take him out of the Glister Academy of Magicks, while his mother insisted he stay. It was nerve-wracking. But Master Shoji always reassured him he would be able to finish his course of studies.

Adler sighed. Missives from his parents were rarely good news unless it was the quarterly missive that held his allowance. It was a month and a half until the next quarter.

He poured his potion into several small blown glass bottles and sealed them with wax. Then he put away the ingredient and washed out the cauldron with fine sand and clear water.

Drying his hands on a rag, he left the room and unbelted his wings. Though he was a gifted apprentice, without the belt to contain his wings, he caused accidents in the small still room. Confining them with the thick belt was the safest option to avoid disaster.

It was a warm day for early spring, a pleasant day to work in the garden. Master was there, as was Mistress Shoji, who was planting seeds in the newly turned soil. Her deer hooves were grimy; she had plowed the rows with her hard hooves. The Shoji's were both tiny in stature but commanded huge respect. Adler often thought on that. It was all about their attitude. He hoped to be able to command respect the same way someday, instead of the blustering criticisms and threats his father employed.

Master Shoji sat on the bench under a blossoming cherry tree, with two letters sitting next to him.

Adler stretched his wings, feeling the kinks caused by the confining belt leave. Later he would take a vigorous flight. He preferred to squat rather than sit on benches, so he sat down on the ground. He was large, heavy, and had been known to break chairs and benches.

With a sigh, he picked up the letters. He opened his father's first.

Dear Son,

I am writing to instruct you in your familial duty. It is my desire that you marry forthwith. I wish you to marry a woman from outside our fair Shire. The Bridal Faire will soon convene in the King's City, with young people from all over the country. I desire that you go there and find a bride. Upon your proof of your marriage — a letter from Master Shoji will suffice as proof— I will bestow upon you six hundred guilders of gold coin and Hill Farm. Blue Flax Farm on the northern border will also be yours, as you know, though you will need to rebuild the house if you wish to live there. For your bride, I will gift a string of fine beads, the workmanship of the Northern Lesser Giants. This will be given to her when you come to visit us at Goldhawk Stronghold. I will also bestow a gift upon the Academy and the tuition for your final year, including your wife's room and board. Your quarterly allowance will increase by ten guilders so you may care for your bride.

Your Expectant Father,
Lord Goldhawk
High Karl, High Reaches Shire
Goldhawk Stronghold

Adler stared at the letter in shock. Marriage? This year, before he was even out of school? He handed the letter to Mistress Shoji, who read it quickly with Master Shoji peering over her shoulder.

He had always known he was expected to marry outside his Kind, the griffintaurs. His family, like all the people of the Elvanor, followed the Old Ways, where each third child married into another Kind. He had two older sisters who were happily married to other griffintaurs, raising families of little fliers.

As the Olde Ways taught, he would marry outside his Kind to keep the lands and people fertile. His children might be griffintaurs, or they might take after their mother and be whatever she would be, a faun or a Lesser Giant or whatever.

He always assumed he would marry into one of the Lesser Giant families along the northern border of his father's land.

"Bridal Faire! Why do I have to go to that now? Why doesn't he wait until I am done with my training? I'll be done in a year!" He frowned. "And what happened to that Lesser Giant girl, Bufflindia? I thought that was all but settled. My mother was sending over a marriage contract to Buf's father."

"Not to speak ill of your Lord Father and our main benefactor here at the Academy, but decisions like that cause one to wonder if he is perhaps sun touched," Mistress Shoji said tartly, handing Adler back the letter.

Adler tossed the letter onto the grass. "Why not find a third daughter at some nearby estate and tell me to marry her?" He grumbled. "If things didn't work out with Buf, there are lots of other girls. It would be quicker, and I don't want to travel!"

Herbs and Potions were his weakest subjects; he had resolved that this spring he would master the subjects.

"No doubt your father has once again antagonized all his neighbors and this is his way of telling them all he doesn't care," said Master Shoji.

"No doubt." Father had a long history of annoying everyone.

Adler ripped open his mother's letter, from which two fat gold coins fell. Crowns, not the usual guilders. More money than his quarterly allowance. He read it aloud.

Dearest Adler,

I am sure your father's command has come as quite a surprise to you. I myself am not sure what to think about it. No doubt a girl from outside our Shire will make a lovely wife, though I had hoped you would marry into that mining family on the Ock

Heights. You'd do fine with a Lesser Giant wife, since you are so large. Bufflindia always seemed so jolly and her family creates such fine jewelry.

Well, it is not to be. Try to pick someone who seems intelligent and who is not too outlandish in behavior. Of course, I will welcome whomever you choose.

For the goodness sake, buy some decent clothes for your journey, don't take those stained work tunics all you apprentices wear!

Your Loving Mother,
Lady Mirilia Goldhawk

"Well, you'd best be getting ready now," Mistress Shoji said, shaking out her apron. "I'll take your measurements and send them to the tailor on the wind. You will have to pick them up before you leave. Good thing you can fly, I hear many of the streams are still in flood and roads are muddy. You have seven days until the festival. It starts on Starday."

"Seven days! Seven days and I look for a wife. The Faire lasts seven days, so in less than two weeks I'll be married to some strange girl. And all I need to know is that she's not from my home Shire. Or a griffintaur, of course," Adler mumbled. "Because my Father argues with everyone."

"Well, he has always been demanding. Good thing your mother has good sense, or you would have turned out just like him." Mistress Shoji stabbed her trowel into the dark soil.

Adler scowled. He did have a temper, but nothing like his father's.

Mistress patted him on the shoulder. "It won't be so bad. There won't be many griffintaurs there. You might be quite popular," she said. "The year my sister Durlene—she's number six, the baby— went to the Bridal Faire, there were only two griffintaur boys. She tried to catch their eyes, but one married a centaur, and one a Lesser Giantess. Durlene ended up marrying a snow faun— they are related to Piper's family, you know. His family had never met an antlered faun before, and thought she was so exotic."

Adler ran a hand through his hair, trying to think of a way to get out of this until he was done with school. He was cursed with wiry golden curls. However, if he angered his father, there might be no school.

"Really, you must let me trim your hair before you go, it is looking quite wild. You will want to appear civilized when you meet all those girls. They travel in from all areas of the country. Buns from the south, centaurs from the plains..."

He paused in his fuming, distracted by the thought of centaur girls. "Centaurs girls— do a lot of centaur girls go to the Faire?" He raised his eyes with interest. Centaur girls were always so—

"No centaur girls!" Master Shoji said sharply. "Where would we put her? We already have you and Pondo. No giant girls, either. Pondo will be bringing his new wife next fall and I have no idea how we are going to fit them in. We're going to have to spend a month building quarters. Get a faun girl or a bun, and you can have the top of the north tower. We'll put up a wall and door for privacy while you are away."

Adler pushed up his spectacles, hoping the movement would distract them from seeing his suddenly flushed cheeks as he had a quick thought about what would be done in the privacy of married quarters.

"I've never even seen a bun girl."

Buns mostly lived south of the Frostmere Sea on the larger continent, and Adler's family lived in the far northeast, not far from the border of Hobb.

"You'll like 'em," Master Shoji said. "They are—" he moved his hands in two rounded shapes, indicating womanly curves. "But make sure you get a big one. Some buns come in tiny size."

"You definitely don't want tiny," Mistress Shoji agreed. "Difficult deliveries, with a husband your size. Though I know some woodwitches that can help in those circumstances. Still, find a nice big girl. But not too big. One who can sleep in the loft."

"Medium sized," Master Shoji said. "Now, get busy."

"WHAT MAGICKS ARE YOU taking, Adler?" Little Piper, the youngest student, a snow faun with thick white hair cut into a bowl shape popular for little boys, was lying on Adler's bed. He bounced a conjured ball with his hooves as Adler packed. His goat legs were thin and fragile and his alabaster horn nubs barely showed through his thick platinum waves. He stuck around Adler in his free time, since some older boys teased him for his tiny size.

"Not many. Master Shoji gave me a couple of his illusion cones, in case I need something long term for hiding if there are thieves on the road. Plus they're small and easy to carry." He held up a small pouch decorated in magical symbols. "A compass, though I probably don't need it, I'll follow the roads to Norport."

"Oh, and my wallet has a heat spell on it, so pickpockets will get burned. Also, Lofting Elixir. With the roads so muddy I'll get an airboat and loft it back here. Otherwise, it'll take a month to get back here by cart. Unless I find a flier bride."

"Not much chance of that, since you can't marry a griffintaur. There might be those flying centaur girls."

"Master Shoji said no centaur girls, we don't have housing for one."

"Too bad. They always have such big—"

Adler gave Piper a *look*.

"No love charms? Don't you need a love charm?" Harl interrupted. He was a golden horsetail faun, with a flowing mane and tail. His dark blond hair was pulled back in another tail to blend with his luxurious mane. The high ponytail would look ridiculous and girly on any other young man, but it made him look warrior-like. He had hard, tilted dark eyes with lashes the girls all liked. Harl was handsome, arrogant, selfish and in the same year as Adler. He knew much more about battle magicks and about women than any of the other students at the school. Harl gave Adler a sly look. "How are you going to get a wife without a charm?"

"Yes, do you think some girl will just up and decide to be your wife? You need some help." Pondo, a Lesser Giant from over the border, nodded, his eyebrows raised. Pondo had the advantage of looking stupid, with his bulging round eyes and double chin, but he was sharp and manipulative. He was the oldest apprentice, graduating before Midsummer, but he was staying an extra year to work on mastering enchantments.

Harl and Pondo always stuck together and were not Adler's favorite people. Lucky for Adler, Master Shoji had made him Head Apprentice, which gave him an edge.

"I'm not charming some girl into being my wife. That is unethical," Adler growled.

Piper rolled his eyes. "What else you taking?"

"Oh, water purifier drops, some stomach calm. Some of Mistress Shoji's ground pepper mix in case the food there tastes funny."

"No protection charms?"

"No, they take too long to make, and I want to sleep tonight."

"Pretty soon you'll be sleeping in the tower," Harl said with a knowing grin. "Or not sleeping." He waggled his dark eyebrows suggestively.

"Please leave," Adler frowned at the older boys.

"Hey, while he's gone, let's work on a transparent wall spell," Harl said to Pondo.

"Oh, yes. I have heard of a transparent paint spell. That would be just the thing," Pondo agreed as they left. "Though I doubt he'll get a girl worth looking at."

"True. But at least she will *be* a girl."

Adler sighed.

"Don't worry about that spelled paint, Adler. I'm superb at messing things up. They'll make me fetch stuff. I'll contaminate it. That work for you?" Piper bounced his conjured ball up to the ceiling.

"Thanks, Piper. You are an honorable friend."

"Are you going to bring back a pretty one? I hope she is pretty. I hope she bakes honey cakes."

"Well, we'll see what I can find."

"Too bad I'm not going with you. I would be a big help picking out a nice one. I have many sisters, you know. None of them are old enough to marry you, though. Redberry won't be seventeen until July. Too bad." The little faun vanished his toy and jumped off the bed. "Well, I best be off to mess up the transparent wall paint."

Piper tapped away to find the older boys.

Adler packed, cursing his father all the while. He didn't want to marry. Not yet. And how successful would a marriage be, to a complete stranger? His only helpful tip was a recommendation on size—not too big or too small. Any medium-sized woman would do.

How many women wanted to marry an apprentice wizard and live in a small room at a school?

Mistress said the fact he was a griffintaur would make him popular with the women, but he could not imagine that. He'd certainly reached the age of twenty-one without even once being popular with the ladies. Except as a Rockroll partner. He had a powerful roll.

"Your father is the Karl of the whole Shire. One day you will be the High Karl, with lands and the castle. That should count for something," Mistress Shoji assured him.

True, if he wanted a wife with gold lust.

He folded the new clothes up and shoved them into his pack. Mistress Shoji handed him a large packet of foodstuffs.

"I wish I wasn't going alone."

"You will do fine, picking a bride. Look for a girl with more interests than her hair ribbons and young men." She patted his shoulder. "Don't trust a flirt. And I might offer a little woodwitch magic to help clear the way."

Adler's jaw dropped open. He always forgot Mistress Shoji was a woodwitch, well respected for her hearth and home magicks. "You can do that?"

"I can't make a woman fall in love with you, but I can clear away...subterfuges. Very helpful when faced with many new people." She rummaged in her apron pocket and pulled out a little clay jug with a cork stopper. "Two drops a day. Get some fruit—berries will be everywhere this time of year—drip the drops, and eat the fruit. If something or someone is lying or playing a part, or has evil intent, they will smell awful to you. Like old fish guts."

"Thank you." Adler put the small jug in his inner vest pocket, where he kept his money.

"Also, twenty-four-hour firerock. If it rains, your Lofting Elixir will be washed away. This is a nice backup for any airboat fire." Mistress Shoji handed him a canvas bag full of dull gray stones.

"Each one will last a whole day?"

"Certainly! I made them myself."

ADLER BARELY SLEPT and was up before dawn for a quick meal.

"Hurry back," Master Shoji said. "And here is a little gift. It looks like a spice pouch but conceals charmed money. It can't be stolen. You might need it in Norport. A large city like that always attracts the darker elements."

"Yes, my goodness! Look out for pickpockets and thieves." Mistress Shoji gave him a fierce hug, her little round face reaching the middle of his stomach.

"Keep your crossbow close on the road." Master Shoji patted him on the wing.

"I will."

Adler took off with a leap and hard beat of wings, getting high into the cool dawn sky. His pack was a little heavy, and he slid it around to the small of his back, his crossbow slung across his chest on his hip. He headed southwest. He could follow the main road along the Ice River. It eventually led to Norport Bay, on the sea, though he had never traveled that far south before. Master Shoji's school was half a day's journey south of his family lands on the northern border. He'd been to the northern port city of Jorghenbag twice, and to a couple of village markets in the neighboring country of Hobb, where father bought weapons from the Orcs, but nowhere else larger than a village.

He wished he wasn't going alone.

Chapter Two

None of the prospective brides came alone to the Bridal Faire, it seemed. They all had grumpy fathers and downright scary mothers. Norport was enormous and the air smelled like old smoke, sewers, and fish guts. He longed for the clean air and green woods of the Shire.

And it was so boring. Soirées, teas, musicales, dress balls. Adler hated them all. Why couldn't there be a picnic or a fine game of Rockroll? Or a theatrical troupe performing a show? Why couldn't it be fun? Like a Faire at home in the Shire, with mummers and food booths, Rockroll lanes with fierce competitions, ribbon dances and country rounds and no one paying attention to how much ale a young man drank.

Morning calls were finally over. He'd wandered awkwardly through the pavilion and hadn't even spoken to one girl today. Why did they always come in clumps? He'd be all right if he could chat with one without her mama watching his every twitch.

He was terrible at bride hunting.

Adler smelled food from several vendors' stalls. The small market near the docks had plenty of food vendors, so he'd spent little time in the larger market or eateries of Norport. Saved a passel of money and probably avoided pickpockets, too.

So far, he'd had no trouble like that—his trouble was talking to young ladies. He circled around, looking for the fruit vendor. Time for his daily clarity drops, which were telling him this venture was all a horrible mistake. The whole thing stank, like Norport, with its disgusting open ditches. Hadn't they ever heard of underground pipes? Compost fields? All the villages at home had them.

Maybe he should fly back to the Academy and see if his father couldn't repair his relationship with the jeweling giants. He could marry Bufflindia or one of her many sisters or cousins. Bufflindia's mother wasn't scary— she would plant a giant tankard of ale in front of him and challenge him to a game of Rockroll. She'd roar with laughter and pound him on the back when she beat him flat.

He landed at the fruit vendor he'd visited before. The seller was cute, a curvy girl. He thought she was human. He'd seen few humans before, though there had been traders from far south in the Jorghenbag market. They were shaped like tiny giants. She had soft, creamy skin and her eyes were a nice light, golden brown with long, black lashes. She wore her hair under a dull gray turban, but he imagined it was dark and thick since the turban was quite round. When she smiled her teeth were brilliantly white, and she had two deep dimples. Adorable. What he could see of her figure under the baggy dress and apron was feminine but sturdy. Not too small, up to his shoulder at least. She would make Mistress Shoji happy, size-wise. Why weren't there any girls like her at the Faire? All with their prissy dresses and terrifying mothers. The fruit seller spoke in a thick accent he didn't recognize.

"Vat vill you have today, sir?"

He looked over the baskets of berries and secretly checked out her hands. Small, sturdy, dimpled brown hands. No wedding ring.

"I'll take the mixed berries."

She went to get a basket. *I wonder where she is from? They wear turbans in the far south. Maybe she is from the far south.* He also noted that her back view was as enticing as her front view. She handed him the basket, and he noted her hands and forearms were hairless. Silky. Maybe hiding the hair was a southern thing? Like the Northern ice giant wealthy ladies wore transparent scarves over their lower face.

He paid for his small basket and stood aside. He had been eating the fruit while standing around, so he could leave the basket with the vendor. No need to collect a bunch of stuff up in his room. He dutifully sprinkled a berry with two drops of the clarity potion.

"Are you ill?" the girl asked him.

Adler cleared his throat. "Ah, no. An elixir. You know, for robust health."

She looked him up and down, but not in the flirty way that made him uncomfortable. She turned and looked behind her. The old lady that generally sat back in the shade was nowhere near.

"Can I ask you zometing?"

"Sure."

"Vat are you?" She raised her arms and did a little flap move.

It was cute. He grinned. "I'm a griffintaur. Wings and clawed feet of a griffin. Like buns have ears and feet of a rabbit, and fauns have ears and feet of a goat."

She nodded. "Vere I am from zhere are only bun, faun, zentaur. Sirens, mermaids and Fairy, alzo."

"Oh. Are you from across the sea? The Three Realms?"

"No. I am from farzzer south. The desert lands along the Southern Sea coast. Zareemjarem it is called."

"That is a very long way from here."

She nodded and gave a wistful smile. "Yez, zo far from home."

"My name is Adler."

The girl smiled her deep dimples and blinding white teeth making her a stunning sight. "Ayperi."

The old faun woman returned and screeched at the girl. "Girl, get me a fresh bucket of water! This has been sitting for hours! Scoot!" The old woman smacked at Ayperi as she rushed away with the bucket. The old woman smelled worse than the open ditches.

That poor girl. Sounded like her employer was mean. Something wrong with that old hag. Adler stuck around for a little while, eating from different vendors, but Ayperi was busy with baskets and the old faun woman didn't leave the booth. He finally went back to his room.

AYPERI FETCHED A BUCKET of water, not at all dismayed the line to the fountain was long. It gave her a chance to watch the intriguing young man with the golden wings. Whoever had imagined such a being. And he was nice, too. He must be in town for the Bridal Faire. She knew he stayed at the inn down the street, in an upper room. Yesterday she'd seen him fly through his window.

His clothing was very nice. He must come from a wealthy family. His hair was held back by a shiny gold ribbon, not a scrap of leather or twine like most men wore.

How she wished she was part of this Bridal Faire. To meet a young man from a far place, a kind man who wouldn't hit her or reek of dark magic.

At least Lerg was still away on the western coast. He'd been gone for more than a month. She was able to get up early, pick berries for the stall without worry she'd be ambushed while the old woman was asleep. Old Changa was a horror, but she did keep her son away from Ayperi.

Finally, it was her turn. She filled the bucket and balanced it on her head, so much easier than holding the handle in her always sore hands. She detoured around the crowd in a way she would be out of Changa's sight. There was a small tree not far, one she gave a blessing of water to when she could. Maybe that action, and other small offerings she gave as she was able were what protected her from Changa and Lerg, with their dark magic. She knew they kept her for a purpose. And she was still a virgin, even after a year in their captivity.

Ayperi came to the small tree and poured some of the water on its base. "Be blessed, little tree," she whispered. The Alvelders of her home taught her to give blessings or sacrifices to the nature spirits. The spirits would remember her in times of need. So far, she was still alive and healthy. That had to mean something.

As she watched the water soak into the soil she thought of the young man with the wings.
A simple offering of water would not bring big dreams to pass.
She hurried back to the fruit stall.

ON THE LAST DAY OF the Faire, Adler packed his belongings, except for the tunic he would wear to the tea and the old work tunic he would wear home. Tomorrow he would leave as soon as he woke in the morning. No wife. His father would not be pleased.

He headed reluctantly to the large striped pavilion tent for the morning tea. Unless by some magic he met a nice girl today he probably wouldn't even bother with the Ball tonight. Engaged couples would be introduced with much fanfare. Who needed that?

The tea was like all the other socials events. Boring. Young women in frilly pastel gowns giggled and grinned, mothers shot arrows from narrowed eyes. He tried to be sociable for a while, but could barely make himself talk to the young women standing and sitting in groups. Balls were better; at least there was something to do. He wasn't a bad dancer if there was room for his wings.

"I'm out of here. I need of nice mug of ale to wash this insipid tea away." The speaker was a skinny faun with frizzy red hair who stood next to him by the refreshment table.

"Sounds good to me."

Two other young men standing around the table overheard them, and they all decided to find a tavern. Adler spent the remainder of the afternoon rolling rocks and drinking ale. He ate a big meal of beef and bread, well cooked. It was far more fun than anything else he'd done this whole week.

Face it, he told himself. *You are a big failure at wife wooing.*

ADLER LEFT THE TAVERN as the sun was setting. He'd go to bed early and leave for home before dawn. He was no closer to getting a wife than he was when he arrived. Besides, he couldn't imagine even one of the girls he met this week living at the school, helping with meals and the garden, or visiting his family at Goldhawk Stronghold. None of these girls would haggle for fabric and jewels with giants on market day as his mother did. They would expect servants to do everything, but at the Stronghold, everyone had a duty or chore, except for the very elderly or ill. There were servants in the kitchens, laundry, woodlands, and fields, but no one in the Stronghold had personal maids, not even his mother. Many women, older unwed women, and widows of the clan had refuge at the Stronghold. Young women with injuries and disabilities had refuge there also, helping where they could. Blind Julia was known for her fine knitted stockings, for instance. The entire fourth floor was devoted to them, with everything flowery and covered in lace. He avoided it as much as possible, though occasionally he had to take a birthday gift to some elderly relative. They did have good refreshments. The women took turns assisting his mother with hair styling and all the business with gowns.

For the next year, any wife of his would have to put up with Pondo and Harl, plus all the other boys at the school. Not high society living.

Being a third was a pain. His sisters were happily married to local griffintaurs and lived in halls nearby, flying home frequently to visit with their children, who of course were griffintaurs. He, being a third, had to marry outside his Kind, as the Old Laws decreed. And really, he did believe in the Old Laws. Look at the Three Realms. They had outlawed the Old Laws and forbade the marriages of thirds outside their Kind. In a half-century, their birth rate had plummeted. The whole country was now in a state of civil war as some tried to return to the Old Laws and others tried to stop them and keep with the Purification Code. Chaos and violence had the country in constant turmoil.

He was glad that fruit seller wasn't from the Realms, with all that danger. But her situation might not be much better, considering the way the old woman screeched at her. He would go see her before he left.

Back in his small room at the inn, he changed into his older clothes—but not a stained work tunic— and flew above the city, enjoying the fresher air far above. The waves moving in the sea were relaxing, as was seeing ships with colored sails move toward the bay. He let the humiliation of his poor wife hunting skills fall away. Finally, he flew over the small market where he'd been buying most of his meals, though tonight he wouldn't stop at any stalls, thanks to the excellent beef.

Ayperi was loading baskets into a pushcart while the old woman sat within it, screeching. Ayperi grabbed the handles, pushing the cart down the street. Surely she could find a better employer. She walked over rough and broken cobblestones with bare feet that looked far too vulnerable. Humans had feet that needed protection. That couldn't be safe! Walking through the city could leave stone bruises or cuts.

He wondered how far she had to go. The little market was in the south part of the city, near the docks, so it had to be a long way. Unless they bought their fruit from a carter from the country at a market somewhere in town.

Curious, he followed some distance behind them, so they wouldn't notice. But Ayperi pushed the cart through the entire city to the eastern countryside. After a while, she turned onto a muddy path. The pushing was difficult, with the cart constantly sinking into the mud. The old faun screeched at the girl and to Adler's shock, she pulled out a thick piece of rope, knotted on the end, and began to beat Ayperi.

Adler didn't think, he just reacted to the sudden burst of anger at seeing the old hag beat Ayperi. He swooped down to the cart, yanked the rope from the old woman's hands and tossed it far away. Then he grabbed Ayperi under the arms and flew her down the lane, landing in a green meadow in sight of the old woman in the cart. The old woman jumped and waved her fists, her screams of rage could be clearly heard.

A great idea dawned on him.

"Come with me, Ayperi! I am here to find a wife, and life with me would be so much better than life with that old hag."

The girl looked down the way to the furious old woman and bit her lip. "Oh, ye are zo zveet. But I cannot. I vas zold to Madam's zon. I am not free to be your wife."

Sold? Slavery was illegal in Elvanor.

"Where were you sold?"

"In Zyweli."

A port city on a lawless island in the Southern Sea. A pirate haven. Even country folk in the north had heard of the island.

"Well, you're in Elvanor now, and slavery is illegal here. Come with me."

She glanced down the lane to the old woman. "Ye von't get in trouble for taking me from her? She showed me papers that looked zo important. Zhough I do not read your words."

Adler glanced at the elderly faun who was shooting stinging sparks toward them. None reached them, sizzling away in the wet field. She looked far more like a hag than any old faun woman he had ever seen. But wasn't a hag affliction a thing that affected humans and giants? Not fauns? He would have to study that.

But dark magic, death magic could turn even a faun. The sparks smelled rotten, meant to injure. The hag had that horrible stench. The clarity drops at work. He had not studied dark sorcerers extensively but had some basic instruction. They were rare in Elvanor and the neighboring countries.

"No. She lied. You are free here, Ayperi."

She looked up at him, her golden brown eyes glimmering with tears. She glanced at furious faun. The old faun was slowly climbing from the cart into the deep mud.

"Yes, I vill come vit you."

"Is there anything you need to get? From your home?"

"Ah, no. Ayperi own nozing."

Adler got a good grip on her from behind, incredibly conscious of her warm bottom against his groin. *By the Winged gods, I have picked a wife! A wife I like—and she is pretty!* He flapped hard and they were soon aloft. Down below the hag screamed and stomped her feet, causing her to lose her balance in the slick mud. The last they saw of her she was sitting in the puddle. He and Ayperi laughed.

He flew her to the inn and pulled her into the small common room.

"I zhink ze old one vill cause trouble. She iz vile." Ayperi had a worried frown on her pretty face. "Her son, he iz not a good one. He vill be trouble if he can."

"Luckily she is stuck in the mud without you to haul her home. We will leave tonight. Let me get my bag. I will only be a moment, I'm already packed to go." Up in his room, he grabbed the bag and rushed down the stairs, half-afraid his new bride would not be there. But she was still by the door. Her smile was blinding.

"Come. We will get to the big market. I hear during the Faire it stays open until midnight. You need clothes and I planned to buy an airboat for my bride." He once again lofted her into the air, and she giggled deliciously.

"AIRBOAT FIRST," ADLER said, finding a basketeer as the sun set low. "I live in the far north and the roads are muddy. Several rivers are in flood stage, too. With the airboat we will avoid all that."

The market was lit by torches as the twilight deepened. The seller had a small lot with different sizes of airboats and fuel for the fire cauldrons. While they looked at several of the smaller boats, Adler told her about his home. "I have one year left at the school of magic. Master Shoji will have a room fixed for us in a tower. After I am finished with school we will go to my home and I will work for our people. My father is the Karl. The leader of our Shire. Someday I will be Karl. We won't be poor, you will not have to work in a stall or fields."

Adler was thankful his Mother had sent the extra gold, and that he had eaten a week of frugal meals in the market instead of visiting inns which charged exorbitant prices during the Faire.

He had enough for an airboat the size of his big bed at the school, with drawers built into the sides. The sides were a good four feet tall, made of thick woven reed. It came with a quilted pad to roll out for a bed, and a pot, a bucket, lengths of rope and anchors. It also had a tarp cover for rainy weather. The airboat's balloon was a plain gray, not one of the gaudily colored ones. He liked the practical color and furnishings and did not try very hard to get a low price. The vendor was happy to tie a SOLD sign on it and hold it for them while they bought provisions.

Oatcakes, dried fruit, dried beef, cheese, crocks of butter and jam and bread, carrots, potatoes, and some seasonings were the foodstuffs they were able to find. He had a good knife, so they got spoons and forks. Adler was confident he could shoot a pigeon or catch a fish here and there for some variety. He wasn't sure how long a journey would take with the airboat, better to have too much food than too little.

Ayperi needed clothes and eventually they found a small shop. He handed her a small pouch of coins. "Here, go buy some dresses and shoes. We will go north where it is colder, so buy warm clothing. We can have summer things made later from the village dressmaker. Get whatever else you need. A comb, hair ties. A shawl."

Chapter Three

Ayperi raised her eyebrows in surprise. Adler grinned. "I have two older sisters, and they couldn't live without a comb and brush, a mirror and hair ribbons. So get those. While you do that I'm going to find the nearest marriage magistrate. I'll meet you right here." He rushed down the street.

Ayperi clutched the coins tightly, hardly believing this was happening. She was leaving Changa and her frightening son Lerg! She was not a slave in this country. It had not ever occurred to her that there were places where slavery was illegal. It was legal at home as payment for a crime.

She had been stolen from the street, almost a year ago now. Her situation could have been worse if she'd been sent to a brothel. Changa and Lerg, for some reason, wanted to keep her a virgin. For now. That had caused her many sleepless nights, wondering what ritual they wanted her for. Somehow they knew she had sea siren blood—her coral pink hair gave that away—and would not come into her magic powers for three or four years. They were willing to wait that long for her marriage to Lerg.

She had seen their book of magicks. Even though she did not understand the Glister magic, or read the Elvanor words, she could tell the book was depraved. Cruel magic. She often worried that she was not meant to live long after the wedding. But now she was free of them!

The shop catered to working women who needed serviceable clothing and could not afford a seamstress. Ayperi bought practical skirts, made with sturdy, heavy stitched pockets, in dark colors. She picked loose tunics, easy to move in, for her tops. Pretty printed tunics in florals and checks were in darker colors to go with the plain skirts. They would be perfect for her new life. She picked a leather and quilted fabric bodice in dark brown, with sturdy cord laces running up the front, which was made for daily wear. It was cleverly constructed to cradle her breasts so it would be comfortable. It pleased her that it had tiny pockets for money or sewing things, and even a hidden pocket inside for a small dagger. Three unbleached aprons for working, undergarments, socks, a nightgown, and warm dark blue shawl, completed her pile. The store had sturdy boots and work shoes. She picked a sturdy pair of leather ankle boots with strong ties. Shoes! How she had longed for shoes in the city. She grabbed a comb, a tiny mirror and a few ribbon ties for her hair.

She left the shop wearing a dark blue skirt with a dark blue and yellow flowered tunic, covered by one of the ruffled, unbleached aprons. Her old clothing was tucked into the cloth bag she had purchased along with her new things. Adler was not in sight, so she quickly shoved the turban into the shopping bag. The simple comb seemed like such a luxury after using just her fingers for so long. She rebraided her long, coral pink hair and tied the end with a ribbon.

Her hair color was unusual even in Zareemjarem, a legacy of her sea siren mother. While most had blue and green hair, some sea sirens had coral colored hair. Ayperi and all her sisters had hair like their mother. With the shawl covering most of her braid, people would assume she had strawberry blond hair in the torchlight. Finished, Ayperi leaned against the store wall and watched for Adler.

The sun was down and the streets were shadowed now, but still full of people and noise. She could not help but search the street for Changa or her son Lerg. She was still fearful they would catch her. With their unsavory power; who knew what they could do? But surely everything was happening so fast tonight they would not find her. She and Adler would leave town this very night. Plus, in her new clothing, she did not resemble the girl in the tattered gown. Her stomach relaxed as Adler came into sight, moving quickly through the crowd.

He grinned and her heart spread up at the sight of his even, white teeth dimples and strong jaw. She smiled back, warmth flooding her. Lerg was so greasy and his teeth were brown, he made her shudder in disgust. Adler was both handsome and wholesome.

"You look pretty in your new clothes, with your turban off. I thought your hair would be dark!"

"My muzzer is a sea siren, her family has coral colored hair."

Adler fingered her braid gently. "I am glad you found shoes. I know where the nearest magistrate is, and he is right down the street. Why don't we go do that and then get back to the airboat?"

"Yes." Ayperi swallowed hard. She was going to marry a man she just met, but it was sure to be better than her life with Changa. It wasn't the wedding of her dreams, but her dreams had changed so much since her capture. Since Changa and Lerg. Instead of crystal flowers floating in the pool of the Oleander Oasis and, lighting the night, and her mother and sisters' ethereal voices raised in joyous song, she would be married in a crowded, noisy market wearing an apron and sturdy shoes. And she was thrilled.

Hand in hand they rushed down the torch lit street to a brightly lit booth. Only one couple was in front of them.

Adler pulled two rings out of an inner pocket. "I bought them in the village back home. Master Shoji, my teacher, charmed them to fit any size finger."

Few women in the markets wore jewelry. Adler might come from a wealthier background than she originally thought. She was not sure what a Karl was, but it sounded important. There was no time to wonder about the man she was marrying, though. It was their turn in front of the magistrate.

The vows the old man had them recite simply declared that they chose to be man and wife for the rest of their earthly life—Or half-man and wife, as the magistrate said. Adler placed the ring on her fourth finger and it shrunk to fit. Tiny sparkles of Glister rose from it. She slid Adler's onto his finger and Glister surrounded his, as well.

"Sign here. If you can't sign you must place a mark and I will write your name next to it."

"Ayperi, I will write your name in Elvanor script and you can sign after it. Is your name only Ayperi?" Adler asked.

"No, Ayperi of the Coral Sea Clan and Oleander Oasis." Her name was long because her parents had never married, but both their peoples acknowledged her. After Adler wrote she signed her name in the flowing style of her homeland. The magistrate dried the ink with fine sand, rolled it up and sealed it with red sealing wax. Then he wrote their names in a large book.

That was it. Ayperi stared at the rolled paper and the ring on her marriage finger. Something so fast, so easy, and her life was changed forever. For the good. Her heart filled with hope.

"When we get home, we can have an actual ceremony, if you wish," Adler said as they walked back to the basket. "And I can give you a second ring with a pretty stone. We live near Lesser Giants who trade with jewels, so you will have a choice. My mother would like a wedding. That's what my sisters did, though my father signed their marriage papers, so they didn't have to see a magistrate."

"Your father can zign marriage papers?"

"Yes, he is the Karl of the Shire, so local administrative legalities are his responsibility."

Ayperi wanted to ask what a Karl was, but Adler tucked all the bags into her arms. He hoisted her up and flew her back to the airboat. It felt marvelous to be held in those muscular arms and fly over the city. He was a strong man, wide of shoulder, tall. His chest and stomach against her back were firm with muscle. He had a sweet smile. Handsome, with that mop of gold hair and those teeth and dimples.

Somehow, her fortune had changed. She had a promising young husband.

"I THOUGHT WE WOULD fly somewhere out of town and anchor for the night. We can find fields and woodlands with no one nearby," Adler said. "I like to camp some distance from the roads. Safer."

Did Adler expect a wedding night? Tonight? She watched him while he grabbed a bite to eat and tied a rope harness he'd fashioned to the metal rings that held the woven airboat canopy to the basket. She hoped not. It would be better to have a chance to get to know each other a little. And bathe.

"That zounds good." It sounded like they would be hard to find. She still felt moments of panic when her heart leaped, that somehow old Changa or her awful son would find them.

They stored their provisions and clothing away, then she sat on the thick bedding while Adler received instructions from the airboat seller. Adler wore a small crossbow he'd pulled from his pack. It looked like a fierce weapon to her.

"I'll direct the airboat with the rope, much easier than trying to actually steer it with the right wind." He put a black rock into the fuel cauldron. "These are magical, so we won't have to buy or find fuel on the journey. I have lofting elixir, also, which doesn't even need a fire."

He came close to her and took off his spectacles. "Could you stow these somewhere safe? I don't need them for distance." Without them he looked less studious, his eyelashes were thick and long, something she had not noticed with the spectacles on. He looked somewhat wild with that mass of gold curls and the huge golden wings. Wild in a way that made her feel warm.

He then maneuvered the airboat out to the street where they could lift off. Lifting anchor,he started the fire with a chant and a rub, and then the airboat floated. She felt the tug as Adler lifted off, directing the airboat across the city with the rope harness around his waist and shoulders.

Ayperi ate an oatcake and a piece of cheese since she was hungry. She watched the city firelight fade into the darker countryside, barely holding her eyes open. She woke up well before dawn to take care of the old women and pick the day's berries, and fell asleep on her straw mat at sunset.

Soon they were out of sight of the city. The countryside was dark, with stars partly covered by clouds. She rolled out the blankets. Warm and cozy, she drifted to sleep.

THE SOFT BUMP OF THE basket touching down woke her.

"I found a good spot to stay the night," Adler said. "There is a wooded area between this field and the North Road, so we can't be seen by travelers along it. There's a stream, too. I'm starving. I thought I'd eat, and then we can sleep."

"I'll get out zhe food."

He leaped into the basket and sat down next to her, intent on the meal. She handed him one of the loaves of bread with butter, dried meat, and a large slice of cheese.

A man so large eats a great deal, she thought. His wrists and forearms were about the thickness of her ankles and calves, and she had always been considered sturdy in build. Not nymph-like, like her sisters.

That reminded her.

"Zhe magistrate called you a half-man. Are you part griffintaur and part human?"

"No, that just means my form is part man, part beast. Like a faun or centaur. Hardly any humans live in Elvanor. There are giants to the north, who look like humans only bigger."

"Your family won't care that I am not griffintaur?"

"No. We follow the Olde Ways. Every third child marries outside their kind. I have two older sisters, so I am the one to marry a woman who is not griffintaur."

"What about children? Our children?"

"They may be griffintaur, or they may be human, like you. We won't know until they are born."

"Adler, I zhould tell you. In a vay, I am a half-man, too. My father iz an Oleander Oasis fairy. They make water flow in the desert, for crops and fruit trees to grow." She fluffed out her hip-length hair. "Sometimes my hair has blue lights. But my mother is a Coral Sea Siren. I have hair like hers."

"A fairy? And a siren?"

"Yes."

"So you know magic?"

She shook her head, sadly. "Not Glister magic. All my magicks were tied to my home in Zareemjarem. Here I know not zhe plant or zhe animals. We practice Alveld magic. It is different from Glister, I think."

All right. Sounded like a woodwitch. He'd studied fairies but since none lived in the northern reaches the information hadn't stuck.

"My Master at school, Shoji, is a High Mage. And his wife is a woodwitch. I am sure she could teach you the northern ways. They are very kind and wise."

"Oh, Adler!"

His new bride launched herself across the padding and clutched him around his neck, planting kisses all over his face.

She smelled sweet like strawberries. He pulled her tight and slid a hand through her hair, which was fine as a spider web.

He cleared his throat. "We're married. We could... kiss on the lips."

She leaned back and looked suddenly shy. "Yes."

Then she pressed her full round lips to his, and he thought his heart was going to pound out of his chest. Heat rushed through him, and he forgot that they barely knew each other. He pressed his tongue between her lips, and she welcomed it, greeting him with her own small, soft tongue. The kiss caused flames to run through him so that he groaned.

She pulled back and he felt crushing disappointment. The kiss...he had kissed girls before, at local fairs and feasts, but Ayperi was more desirable than any of those girls. Enchanting.

"I vish to please you, be a good wife...but I like to vait. A few days?" Her eyes were wide with apprehension.

He hadn't really expected *that*. "Oh. Certainly, we can wait a few days. We need to get to know each other."

"Though I would like another kiss." She dimpled.

She liked my kiss. He grinned.

They kissed, several long kisses. The heat of them made him tremble, passion rising in his groin, aching for her. He wanted to slide his hands all over her, under her garments, find out if her skin was as silky as it looked, but he restrained himself. This was too new, too precious. He didn't want to ruin it.

They slept, her back nestled against his front, one of his wings spread over her for warmth through the night.

Chapter Four

The next morning Ayperi ran to the stream for a good wash up. Adler packed up the little they had out and then flew high. There were clouds on the horizon, and he wanted to study the air currents.

His vision for distance was sharp like an eagle's. He tunneled his vision and could see something dark against the gray clouds. It was coming from the city. Not an airboat. As he watched, it moved slightly with the air currents, revealing a rectangular shape. A flying carpet? Those took strong magic. He didn't know anyone who used them. They were common in the desert lands, though.

The connection to the desert bothered him. Ayperi had those creepy slaver owners. He rushed down to Ayperi. She was wrapped in a towel and she squealed.

"Sorry. Flying carpet, headed this way. We have a little time. I saw it, probably three miles from here. Someone with strong magic has to fly it."

Ayperi's eyes got huge. "Lerg. The old voman's zon. He has a flying carpet."

Adler grabbed her clothes from a bush and shoved them at her. He pulled her into his arms and got her to the basket. "Get out my pack and crossbow while I lift the anchor." He pulled the anchor spike out of the earth but left it trailing on the ground.

She threw on her clothes and pulled out the pack. He leaped into the basket and pulled out two small objects. "I'll light this illusion cone. We will look like a gray boulder. But we must be quiet. We will wait until they pass—be ready for anything."

Quickly, he grabbed a strawberry from their food drawer and sprinkled the clarity elixir on it. He wanted to see what they were dealing with. Then he strapped on the crossbow.

He lit the cone and the other small stone. The airboat rose a little, a foot or so from the ground.

Adler leaped out and pulled the basket closer to the woods, fitting it into a spot under an overhanging tree limb where the bladder wouldn't get punctured. Adler held a finger to his lips. He grabbed and readied his crossbow, all the while trying to think of defenses against flying carpets. Unfortunately, he had not studied them in Magical Home Defense because carpets were practically nonexistent in the north.

Surely he knew something that would work!

The carpet arrived on the wind, a foul stench preceding it. Adler felt the fruit he just gobbled down try to fight its way back up.

The carpet flew past, and he Ayperi relaxed against him. Then it turned around.

"I know she's around here. I can smell her." The voice was low and harsh.

Ayperi grabbed his arm tightly.

The carpet flew over the trees and Adler realized they did not know about the airboat basket. "They think we are in the woods," he breathed into Ayperi's ear.

Soon the wizards on the rug began shooting energy bolts into the trees. The bolts snapped and sizzled, making a lot of noise and filling the air with the smell of sulfur.

"I'm not sure how to stop them," he confessed softly. "They have power."

"If I vas at home, I would unleash zhe movs," she whispered in his ear.

It took a moment to decipher what she said. *Unleash the Moths. Moths eat fabric.*

Holes in the rug would bring it down. He knew a simple care taking spell to close holes in fabric. What if he reversed it to grow holes?

"I have a plan. I'm pulling you to the field where you can lift. There is a strong wind, the airboat will be caught in it and move swiftly. You will look like a gray cloud because of an illusion I will cast. Stay low and hang on. I'll catch up." He sat the illusion cone on the floor of the basket and change the illusion to a cloud, glad Master Shoji had given him seven. Then he lit a firerock.

He tugged the airboat to the field, wondering if the carpet flyers would notice that the boulder moved. Maybe not, they seemed intent on the woods, where he and Ayperi might be camping if they had walked half the night. Without the anchor, the airboat rose and was soon caught in the wind.

Adler's wings were silent, like an owl's. He flew up behind the carpet. There were three men, shooting miniature lightning bolts into the thickets and trees. Good thing it had been a wet spring or there would be a forest fire.

He whispered to his arrows, an unraveling spell, the opposite of the one he used to darn his socks, glad he had mastered oppositional spells last year. In rapid succession, he shot three arrows into the carpet.

One of the wizards saw him and raised his staff to shoot. Adler dived into the trees, weaving in and out, grabbing trunks to swing around the trees to change direction.

Their carpet was not so agile. There was a scream. He paused by thick tree. The three holes in the rug were now a foot in diameter, the carpet flapped wildly like a sheet in the wind, tossing one wizard high into the air while the other two grasped at the edges, trying to gain control.

Adler headed high into the air. At least one wizard was still able-bodied, a shard of energy whizzed by him, clipping a wing and filling the air with the smell of burnt feathers. Far to the east, he saw the airboat disguised as a small cloud, caught in a fast wind stream. He put his muscle into it and flew like mad to get to her. As he got close she dangled the tow-rope down, and he swooped for it. He pulled up, fighting the wind, until they were free of it, above the stream, above the clouds. It was cold and damp, but safe.

"Are you all right?" He called.

"Yes. Vat about zhem?"

"They crashed. The old woman wasn't with them."

"Magicks? To crash it?"

"Yes. I took your advice and made holes. I hope they don't know how to darn fabric."

Ayperi made a rude sound. "Zhose wizards will not know homey magicks. Zuch work iz below zhem. Lerg will have to take it to his muzzer."

Adler nodded. "At my school, we learn them first year and use them in chores all during our schooling. We'll fly a couple of hours away from the woods and then set down, so we can eat."

Later they landed on a high rocky tableland with the woods and the North Road in the distance. They made a quick meal of cheese, bread and fruit while he got out his compass and a sheaf of paper. "I think we should avoid the road."

"You zhink zhey vill still follow us?"

"Yes. I think they found the marriage record, which has my name and home. If they haven't, they can find it easily enough since it is a public record, and there can't be too many Ayperis getting married. However, they will not know about the school, which is some distance south of my home. We can get there and figure out how to stop them if they come." He looked at her, studying her wide, apprehensive eyes. "That elixir I take, it is to show me the true essence of a person. Liars will stink. Those men smelled like rotting meat. Like death."

She nodded. "I know zhey are evil men. The mozzer and zon, I know zhey vanted me for zometing but zhe time was not right. Zhey did not tell me about their plan. I cannot read your scripts, but zhe old woman had a book. I know it vas evil because I could feel dark magic on it."

Ayperi looked down at her feet. "I am sorry I put you in danger. I did not zhink ve could be followed."

"They got lucky following the North Road because they knew I lived far north, perhaps. All griffintaur live in the north. Or else they used magic..." He thought about it for a while. "Could they have a tracker spell on something of yours?"

Her eyes widened. "My hair cover. Changa make me wear it all zhe time. But I had two dresses and four aprons. Only one hair wrap."

Adler nodded. Cloth could be enchanted in many ways. "I think we should burn your old dress and turban. Perhaps your clothing was bespelled, so he could find you."

He looked at her. "You think there is a reason they want you. A magical reason?"

Ayperi looked down and twisted her apron in her hands. "Perhaps. I am mixed blood. I vill not come into my power until after I turn twenty. Zhe women in my family get powers at twenty or twenty-one. Zhat is common wiz my people. One year or two years from now. I zhink zhey vere hiding me until zhen." She looked up at him, her eyes once again light brown in the daylight. "I do not know vat zhey vanted of me. But it was evil. A dark working."

He patted her knee. "Master and Mistress Shoji know many things about magic. We will talk to them. When do you turn twenty?"

It struck him, he was married to a woman, and he didn't even know her birthday, or how many brothers and sisters she had.

"Zhe monz are not zhe same here. My birthday here is mid-winter. But it is mid-summer at home."

"So it will be some time." He stood, and pulled her up by her hands, making her giggle as he lifted her briefly off the ground. "I will make the fire."

She nodded and dragged out her old clothes, and they made a fire pit and burned them. While they did that Adler studied the compass and made a few notes on paper, which he stowed in his traveling vest pocket.

AYPERI WATCHED THE skies anxiously as they lifted. She knew Adler had long distance vision, but she couldn't relax. The carpet was destroyed, but perhaps Lerg had another plan.

Adler towed the airboat some miles east of the road and then headed north. He zigzagged and backtracked. Ayperi could not keep track, though occasionally she saw the road. The terrain below them changed as the day progressed, becoming hills and eventually rock cliffs and outcrops, highlands that lead to the snow-capped mountains in the distance. Adler did not stop for lunch; she handed him bread and apples as he flew by.

At dusk, they landed in a small meadow on the side of a mountain. "We made good progress because the wind was behind us. We are now in the Glisters, a northern mountain range. I plan to fly east from here and then drop south to the school. Anyone trying to follow us will go first to my family's hall. The family wizard there, Jolan, is wily. And my father's guards are Lesser Giants, centaurs and griffintaurs. A mighty force."

Ayperi had never seen a giant, but if they were larger than Adler or a centaur then they must be fierce.

Adler anchored the basket, and they started a campfire using his firerock charm. Ayperi set a pot of water from the stream to boil.

"I am setting an illusion cone. I don't really think we could be followed, but I think we'll both sleep better knowing we are hidden." Adler lit the cone and whispered to the small flame. "We look now like a group of shrubby pines."

Ayperi got food out. "How about roasted potatoes vit cheese and dried meat?"

Adler grinned. "Can I have four? I'm starving."

He rubbed his shoulder. "Arms are tired from all the zigzag pulling I did against the wind this morning."

Ayperi grabbed a blanket. "Stretch out on the grass vhile I get dinner going. You should rest."

She scrubbed the potatoes, placed them in one of the pots, and set it on the edge of the fire.

"Here, eat some fruit and dried meat. It vill be some time before zhe potatoes are done."

Adler flopped back onto the blanket with a groan. "I know there is fish in that stream but I think I'll wait until morning to catch a couple. We'll have a good breakfast." He yawned and closed his eyes.

Ayperi left him to nap.

They ate the plain meal of potatoes with butter, cheese and dried meat. Adler helped her wash the dishes in the stream. They drank tea in front of the fire as the dusk turned to dark night. Clouds had blown in, blocking the moon and stars.

"It might rain. I'll get that canvas cover up," Adler said.

They could stay cozy and dry through the night. Another night pressed to each other, all night long. Maybe more of those long kisses....maybe more. Adler's heart sped up.

They got their few chores finished as icy cold raindrops poured down on them. Inside the basket, Adler adjusted the canvas roof so rainwater would run off. In the light of a tiny lamp Ayperi unrolled the bed and got the blankets spread out.

"Hopefully the rain will end by morning, and we can continue on our way," Adler said. He eased onto the bedroll behind her, trying to keep his breathing normal so Ayperi wouldn't think he was strange.

"Adler?"

"Yes?"

Ayperi rolled over to face him. He dragged in a deep breath as her breasts rubbed against him.

"Ve must talk."

Adler wondered if she could feel his erection against her hip. He sure could. "Um. Sure. It's just— I find it hard to concentrate like this."

"Cloze togezer like this?"

"Yes."

She nodded. "Me, also. But, is important. I vas not planning to marry, Adler. Zo I did not visit a midwife."

He frowned. "Visit a midwife?"

It was her turn to frown. "For herbs? Most young brides take herbs for a vhile zo no babies right away."

"Oh! Yes. Here in the north, you would see a woodwitch. Mistress Shoji is one."

"I vill talk to her. To not have babies right away?"

Babies. Adler's stomach tightened and thoughts of passion evaporated. He hadn't even thought of such a thing. Children were years in the future when he was established as the Shire wizard. And to appease his father her might learn some battle magicks. His mind painted a picture of him trying to study alchemy equations at the table in the loft with screaming babies everywhere.

"Oh, yes. We will be living in the loft for a year while I finish my schooling. Then we'll go home and I'll work with our Shire wizard for several years. There is so much to learn. I have a suite of rooms in the Stronghold, and there is a fine nursery there, also. Or we can move into a house when we leave school. Very nice but not really large. Fine for a small family. The Stronghold would be safer and less isolated, though."

Ayperi patted his chest. "Yes, I am pleased to vait."

"I wasn't planning to marry this year," he confessed. "I planned to wait until I was done with my final year of school. But my father demanded I marry."

He sighed. "He wasn't too thrilled that I went to the Wizard School, he wanted me to learn battle magicks…But in a few years, our Mage will retire. The Shire needs a Mage. I showed talent early, too. I was afraid he might cut off my schooling if I didn't get married as he ordered. But then I met you."

"Oh, Adler. I am sorry ve didn't get to court and get to know each ozzer. Zhere is so much we don't know about one anozzer. But I am glad to be free of the old voman and her son. You are a good man I can tell. I want to be a good wife to you." She snuggled her face against his shoulder as thunder roared outside their shelter. "Ve must make the best of it."

He stroked her silky hair. "Yes, we will make the best of it. I have a good feeling about this marriage."

"Me, too," Ayperi whispered while she slid her arms around his neck. "You are kind and handsome. A good man, too. I can tell." She pressed her soft lips to his and Adler thoughts were suddenly far away from howling babies and his ornery father. Their kisses grew more heated. The kisses made him feel wild, bold.

"I want to see you. Without this," he whispered, tugging at her bodice. He felt his face turn red and was glad for the dim flickering light.

She giggled. "It is night."

"Not when there is lightning."

"All right. Only my top. Ve vill save the bottoms for later. But you must take off your shirt, too."

"Yes." He scrambled out of his tunic and then helped Ayperi with the laces on her bodice. Soon the tunic was over her head, soft skin against him, the hard tips of her nipples pressing his chest. He prayed for lightning and was soon rewarded with a glimpse of high, full breasts and pink nipples that drew his fingers like iron to lodestone.

"You are so beautiful," he whispered against her lips.

"You are too, my husband. Very strong." Her fingers slid over his abdomen, and he sucked in his breath, wanting her hands lower.

"Chop wood, haul water," he said, though his voice was raspy now. "It is a phrase Master Shoji says often to the apprentices, especially if they are fighting."

Ayperi giggled.

"There is much ve can enjoy before I go to woodwitch," she whispered in his ear. He grunted an agreement as his mouth found her nipples, giving her long suckling kisses. Then one small, strong hand slid to his breeches, loosening the laces. He was paralyzed. Her hand was so small and warm. He could barely breathe. She encircled his length. He groaned, incapable of speech and then kissed her, a fierce meeting of tongues, while he pulled her tight, his hands finding her round bottom still in thin drawers.

His ability to think, something he prized in himself, was gone, torn away by the pleasure of a small hand on his cock. Her scent, like sweet berries, surrounded him as he buried his face in her silky hair. He gasped, occasionally tonguing her neck as he came with the next lightning strike.

SOMETIME IN THE NIGHT the thunderstorm ended, and he threw back part of the canvas topper so that dawn's light woke him. They were a tangle of limbs, one of his wings covering her from shoulder to thigh to keep her warm. Ayperi woke as he sat up, her eyes a warm gold in the soft morning light.

"I was going to fly over to the stream to wash up." His eyes could not leave her naked breast, viewing her for the first time in good light. Stunning. "Take me vith you." Ayperi grabbed towels and the soap and his razor from one of the drawers and stuffed them in one of the shopping bags. He grinned enjoying the sight of her in the nearly see-through drawers, packing their things so calmly. He pulled her into his arm, back to front and rushed through the cool air to the stream, wishing they had time for more than a wash-up. In the stream, she was completely naked, and he got glimpses of her sweet triangle and bottom as they scrambled in and out of the water. They washed each other, giggling alternating with hot kisses and then rushed back to the airboat and their clothing.

"I will cut bread and cheese."

"All right. I want to fly high and see what might be happening along the road."

There were no travelers along the road because the mud was formidable. Adler suspected many travelers would spend the next few days waiting in the city for the roads to dry before they attempted more travel. No signs of the carpet, or any other airboats.

He swooped down to the airboat where Ayperi was stowing the bedding and told her the good news. "We are well away from them, I think."

Ayperi shrugged. "Carpets are not good in rain, I doubt they could get to us now."

"No, and if they do get to my father's land...well, his defenses are strong." Adler lofted the airboat with the elixir, and they headed for home. He was returning with a bride, a beauty with a good heart. Piper would like her. All the boys would. And Harl would be green with envy.

Chapter Five

A few more days of calm travel brought them to a land of forest covered hills with meadows in the valley and a shining stream. "The school is not far. We should be there by lunch," Adler said.

"There it is." Adler pointed to a large wood and stone building in a sunny valley. The hills surrounding the valley were pine woods forests, a tree that did not grow in Ayperi's homeland. "It is called a lodge and is made of logs and stone. The boys live on the third floor, but I think we will have a room in one of the towers." Two stone round towers flanked the building.

Adler lowered the airboat to just above the trees, and they entered a meadow. The lodge before them had a steeply pitched roof of red tiles and the window shutters and front door were painted a soft red. The second floor had a balcony facing the south, with wooden furniture. A few young boys sat outdoors playing a game with sticks. They waved wildly when they saw the airboat.

"The towers have a great view and are used for fire watch in the summer."

"It is lovely." And orderly. There were stone fenced garden areas, orchards, padlocks, a barn, and sheds. A place where a foundation was in the process of being fitted with stone walls. Young boys running after each other and a ball in a grassy meadow. A large pond in the meadow had a bench and a small dock. Horses, gnarlhogs, cows, sheep and chickens were in the pastures and farmyard.

"Looks like they started on the new housing. Pondo is also getting married and bringing his bride here. They are Lesser Giants, so Master Shoji decided to build housing for them."

They landed on a green lawn in front of the house, two fat sheep staked nearby working to keep the grass low. Adler set the anchor and helped Ayperi out of the boat.

A small man and woman, the antlered fauns Adler had told her about, came out the front door, round brown faces wreathed in smiles. They were both dressed in dark brown robes, serviceable clothing. Mistress Shoji wore a half apron with numerous pockets,

Deep inside, Ayperi knew she was safe. She could feel warm homey magicks, like a freshly made loaf of bread, surrounding her in comfort. This was so much better than the old woman and her evil son.

"Master Shoji, Mistress, I would like to introduce my bride Ayperi, from the land of Zareemjarem."

"My that is so far away! Welcome to the Glister Academy of Magicks! Why don't you come in, we will have lunch in our private parlor and get acquainted," Mistress said. "Taryn, why don't you and the other fourth-year boys carry their belongings to the new room. Come, I will show you the lodge."

They walked into an entryway with a parlor with cushioned furniture in greens and dark reds. "This is the reception parlor, mainly used when families visit, or for quiet reading." The next room, which was through a door on the back wall, was huge, the rest of the ground floor, Ayperi surmised. A kitchen with a large stone fireplace and an iron oven were against the back wall which had windows overlooking the garden area. The walls and floor were polished wood, as were the peeled log rafters. in front of the fireplace was a thick woven area rug in green, red and brown, with several chairs and couches arranged around it. A long dining table with bench seats filled the area next to the sitting area. Flowers and apple blossoms in a clay jug sat in the middle of the table.

"This is the main living area, we call it the Common Room. We eat meals here, the students study or play games. They help with the kitchen chores, but I do most of the cooking with help from the students.

"The staircases lead to the second floor, which is the classrooms. Third floor holds the dorm rooms and bathing areas. The towers are accessed by the doors near the staircases, they are separated from the second and third floors. Shoji and I have the south tower. Master Shoji's office and library are above our private rooms. The north tower holds a common room for the teachers, a library for the students and your room at the top. We will show you after lunch. There is the farm, of course, and the teacher's cottages."

She opened the back door. "The stillroom and the greenhouse, and the yard. We grow much of our food. It is good for the boys to work physically."

"It is so homey," Ayperi said.

They followed the Shojis to their dining parlor on the ground floor of the south tower, a sunny room with a dining table and a window full of plants.

A meal was brought in by an older boy with a friendly grin. He was like a faun with two legs, but had horse's hooves and horse-like legs and ears, plus the hair on his head was like a full horse's mane. He had a horse's tail, a shiny dark brown color. His eyes were dark with an exotic tilt.

"This is Marcil, a Horsetail Faun from the eastern mountains. Like the Griffintaurs, and antlered fauns like my dear wife and I, they are unique to this area of the world." Marcil placed a platter of roasted chicken onto the table. He left and returned with roasted vegetables and bread and butter. A finely carved sideboard held plates, flatware, napkins, and taps with wine or ale.

"Marcil can bring hot herbal tea, if you would prefer it."

"I will take water." Adler had the ale.

"Tell us about your home," Mistress Shoji said after the food had been passed.

"Zareemjarem is very hot. It is on the coast of the Great South Sea. No snow. No mountains. Desert land with sand and small bushes. Many farms and orchards along the Great River, the Soss. In Zareemjarem we have the faun, centaur and buntaur. Also the Desert Fae at the oases, and sirens near the sea."

"Fascinating," Master Shoji said. "We have Dwarves throughout the land, mostly Black Dwarfs. Lesser Giants live beyond the northern border. They do not live in a Glister land and magic is not a large part of their lives. Across the eastern mountains, The Jaggins, is the land of Hobb. Orc lands, though many others live there also. Beyond Hobb there is a country called Emrysdell which has even more types of peoples, plus intelligent animals who can speak in a way. It borders the Dawn Sea. Hobb is a Glister Land but Emrysdell only has Glister along its western mountain range, the Shards. They have different magic along the coast, similar to the Lesser Giants. Ritual magic, amulets, shamans."

"There are other countries to the south of us that had Glister magic, but it seems to be dying in those lands. We don't know why."

"I will show you a map we have in a school room," Adler said.

"I vould like to see zhat." There were so many things about this land she wanted to learn. "My home has no Glister. It has Alveld. Some work Alveld for potions and other workings. I had not seen the sparks until I came here. But zhere is magic at home. My father calls zhe waters, to make zhe desert bloom. All the Fae do. Some Sirens can see ships foundering at sea, and can save zhem and bring them to zhe land. Zhe sailors then owe a debt to the sirens."

"I have heard of sirens. But the stories told are not flattering."

Ayperi put her bread down. "My mozzer is a siren, a coral siren. She sings; her singing can heal or harm. But she is not wicked. Some sirens are wicked. They make slaves of the sailors. Adler said you do not have slaves in the Elvanor."

"Glister can be used to help or harm, also. Intent is all." Master Shoji said. "So your mother is a siren, and your father is Fae?"

"Yes. They are not married because the Fae Prince can only marry fae, by order of their queen. But zhat is not scandalous in Zareemjarem unless they abandon their children. Zhe fae do not abandon their young. My fazzer loves my sisters and me."

The all paused to eat for a while.

"I heard the south has different plants and animals," Mistress Shoji said, passing a plate of small fruit tarts.

"Zareemjarem is a hot, dry land. The South Sea borders to the west. North is the Empty dessert. Some people do live there, but there are no villages. The Soss River flows through to the sea. Land is good for growing by the river. Zhere are orchards of pomegranates, olives, figs and oranges that are not here in Elvanor. Or lemons. Our bread is thin." She held her thumb and finger up indicating a small space.

"I notice your hair is of a different color than we see here in the north. So the humans have bright hair there?" Mistress Shoji asked."

Ayperi smiled, with her dimples showing. "Most of zhe humans have dark brown skin and hair. Zhey are thought to be handsome people, zheir clothing is bright colors. Zhey follow gazelle herds though the highlands for zhe hunting. They live in cloth and animal skin houses, and travel with horses, oxen, hogs, and goats.

"Near the oases and rivers are orchards and farms. The Desert Fae live at the Oases. All land people farm. Fae, human, buntaur, zentaur, fauns. Sirens live by the sea. The ports are busy with markets and travelers."

Ayperi took a bite of a strawberry tart and then spoke some more. "My muzzer is part Coral Sea Siren, part human. She sings at an inn at the port. The Coral Sirens all have hair zhat is pink, purple, orange, red. Like the ocean coral. My oldest sister Kiralla has bright coral pink hair, I am more dark pink, and my sister Zuhanna is pale pink, almost white. She is older zhan me. I wonder if she has her magic talent now? My sister Kirella has Siren singing abilities. My little sister Adrina is too young to have a talent, as am I. Her hair is like mine. My fazzer is the Prince of the Desert Fae. He is dark with black hair and blue eyes. Oleander Oasis is his home. My sisters and I traveled between both parents."

"So, tell us how you met."

"I ate in the market rather than in the taverns most of the time." Adler said. "She sold berries in small baskets. We got to talking. She was much easier to talk to than the young women at the Faire events. Her employer did not treat her well. I saw the old hag beat her with a heavy rope, and flew her away."

"Zhe old woman has a bad zon. He followed on the carpet. Dark magicks."

"They want her for some reason. Perhaps a power they think she will have?"

"They might want a siren to sink ships for them." Ayperi shuddered. "Or for a ritual. Zhey reek of evil magic."

"I can see that a magical talent like Far Moving could be exploited," Master Shoji said.

"Yes. Zhat is our history. Our clan does not tell of our powers to outsiders. And our homes are strong. I vas stolen in the market. I vas with my sisters. I do not know if zhey were taken too."

"I will study on a way to get a message to your father in Zareemjarem. We will speak of your dangerous encounter on your journey here after supper, with the older students present," Master Shoji said as Marcil cleared the table. "They will need to be alerted. I will contact Adler's father so his garrison can be on the watch. There is not much for the garrison to do right now since those northern dwarfs were defeated two summers ago up on the north border. It has been peaceful."

As they left the room after finishing lunch they followed Mistress Shoji to their room. "Until dinner why don't you rest and refresh yourselves. You have a tea kettle in your room and I believe we stocked oatcakes and tea for you. I am certain you will not have a moment's peace once you join the students. Piper missed you terribly."

Adler grinned. "He is a character, isn't he?"

THE SHOJIS WERE AS kind as they were intelligent and Ayperi was filled with delight as she and Adler were shown their new room.

"Mistress Shoji, could I speak with you about marriage things? Alone?" Ayperi asked quietly.

"Certainly. Join me in the still room."

"I vill be right back, Adler," she told him. He grinned and stretched out on the large bed.

The still room smelled of herbs and fresh soil. They sat on a small bench.

"Adler and I vould like to have no baby until Adler is done vis his studies. I do not know where to find a potion for zis."

"I understand entirely, it will give you two time to get to know each other. And Adler was very surprised his father wanted him to marry before school was over, so no plans were made ahead of time for housing or anything. I do hope that room will work. His father is an impulsive man. A good man but quick to make decisions, and sometimes he makes them without thinking of consequences." She patted Ayperi's arm. "Adler will be Karl one day, what if he'd found a horrible wife?

It could affect the whole Shire. He did well in finding you, I can already tell. I will teach you to brew the potion tomorrow morning. But it will take a month to work, a full moon cycle. 'Tis the way of fertility. Not easy to suppress in the young."

"Zhank you!"

AYPERI LOVED THEIR room. It was in the round north tower and had windows in four directions. A fireplace was between two windows and a tall wardrobe between two others, with a small bathroom enclosed. A large cozy bed (Adler told her it was a sleigh bed) was covered with a down mattress and a puffy, colorful patch quilt. Under a window a table sat with two stuffed blue chairs, and bookshelves filled all other wall spaces.

"This is nice," Adler jumped on the bed which did not move or squeak. "My parents must have sent this down. The dorm beds are horsehair mattresses on ropes frames. The quilt looks like something the women of the Stronghold made, so it will have warming charms in the winter. And we don't have to share a bathroom."

The closet contained a small toilet and there was a brass bathtub against a wall. "Yes, zhis is nice. Lovely. But hauling water for ze bath will be a problem with all zhose stairs."

Adler grinned. "You forget I am a wizard. I can summon water from the well, heat it in the tub and even make the tub larger."

Ayperi climbed up on the high bed next to him. "Large enough to share?"

"Oh, yes."

He pulled her close for a kiss. "A nice steaming bath would be good after our long journey."

He enlarged the tub and summoned water while she searched the closet and found towels.

"I talked to Mistress Shoji about zhe birth control charms. She knows a good one she can teach me to make tomorrow. A potion. I am going to help wit zhe cooking and chores and zhat way Mistress Shoji will teach me to read Elvanor script and do charms."

Adler turned to look at her, "I never thought of that, that you didn't know how to read our language."

"It is important I learn, Adler."

Adler set up the tub large enough for two and filled it with heated water. While he did that Ayperi lit a small fire. Spring afternoons were still cool. "It's ready," he said, his voice raspy.

Ayperi came to the tub, walking with a graceful sway. She had never been naked with a man before, though Adler had seen more than enough on their journey. But it was common to bathe with the family in thin bathing gown that fell above the knee, so it didn't seem that strange to undress. Her hair was in a braided knot at her nape. She unbraided it and fluffed it out. Then with no pretense, she stripped off all her clothes and carried them to the wicker laundry basket.

On their journey, Adler had glimpses of her before, but now he could look his fill. Her bottom was perfect. Silky skin round globes shaped as a human woman, like the Giants in form. Two dimples at the base of her spine. Her legs were firm and well muscled and formidably strong. He was glad for that, it gave her some protection. Her skin was so soft, even on her feet. He felt a need to protect her with good garments. Maybe charms...

His brain seemed to freeze at the sight of her breasts in the day lit room. How had he ever found a wife this beautiful? He breathed out loudly and she looked up at him. "Beautiful." He couldn't get enough of the round fullness that moved as she walked and leaned over, her nipples dark coral and pointed. He thought she was adorable and stood frozen and aching hard at such perfection. He wanted to say something more, about how he hadn't expected such loveliness but his brain couldn't help him form the words. Ayperi walked to the tub. She was not the least bit shy. That was a little shocking. He expected a girl to be shy. "I thought you'd to be shy," he finally said.

Ayperi slid into the tub and held her hand out for him. She wasn't quite smiling.

"I grew up around a pool in zhe family courtyard. All our rooms open to it. It is very hot in Oleander, our home in Zareemjarem. We could not live in the royal palace, but fazzer made sure we had a comfortable home. When we wear clothes in our home they are thin, see-through except for lady parts."

His hands went to the ties at his shoulders. Because of his wings, all his tunics were step-ins that tied at the shoulders, cut in the back so his wings had freedom of movement. He stepped into the tub, face a bit red to be seen naked, with his erection jutting out. Then she slid her arms around his neck. "Ve can't make love until after the next full moon. The potion must work through a moon cycle."

"That is perfect because I won't have classes. It will be the Midsummer Moon. We will be at my parents, which is lovely, and my suite is private. We'll have more time to be alone together because we will have no chores or studies," Adler spoke the words into her hair.

"It will be my first time. Will it be yours, Adler?"

"Yes. I have kissed girls at Fairs and country dances, but that is all. I knew my parents planned to choose a bride. They had a group of young men for my sisters to pick from, I thought they would do the same. I did not try to meet young women though I kissed some at dances."

"I like that we are virgins togezzer and will share our first time."

"Me, too." He pulled her onto his lap. "But until then we can still enjoy each other."

Chapter Six

"Does all your family have pink hair?" Piper asked at dinner, causing a few students to choke on their food.

Ayperi smiled at the little white-haired faun, amused. He was so cute. "My sister Kirella has brighter coral hair and my sister Zuhanna has pale pink hair, almost white. My baby sister Adrina has hair just like me, pinker than Kirella but darker zhan Zuhanna."

"How old are they?"

"Kirella is twenty-one, Zuhanna is twenty, I am eighteen and Adrina is only fourteen."

"I have sisters too. Redberry is seventeen, Blueberry is sixteen, the twins Pinkberry and Lilacberry are thirteen and Snowberry is three. We are snow fauns, our hair stays white all the time."

"How lovely. Ve do not have snow in my homeland. Fauns in our land are tans, golds, blacks and browns."

"What kind of houses do you live in? I live in a wooden house made of logs. Like the lodge but no balcony or towers."

"We live in houses made of brick from the desert sand or from stone. Dig, cut big stones."

"We call that a quarry."

Ayperi smiled. "My fazzer's home is white stone with blue lines."

"Do you have magic where you are from?" Pondo was surprisingly polite. She had expected him to be rude, but he had been raised with manners, it seemed. He was huge, two heads taller than Adler, taking up the width of two men at the table. He had a special bench, extra thick. His hair was dark blond, features ordinary, jaw broad. His own wedding was very soon, perhaps he had decided it was time to act like a man, not a schoolboy.

"Yez, Pondo. But not the Glister. I can raise the sparkles here but not at my home. Glister is not known. I have training in my home, from my fazzer and grandmozzer. They are desert fairies. My fazzer's family has protected Oleander Oasis for long, long time. They do magic called Alveld. They give offerings to the Elders. But I do not know your ways or plants. Ve use magic crystal, found in the sands, but I do not zhink those are used here. All is different."

Adler's other age mate, Harl, was quite handsome, though his face had a permanent smirk she didn't like. He was not so polite, roving his eyes over her body. He was a horse tail faun. His mane of hair was dark blond, shaved in a way that it looked like a mane that matched his tail, and eyes were dark brown. He was as tall as Adler, but of thinner build, except for his horse-like legs which looked very strong. He did not say much.

"Did you go to lots of dances at the Bridal Faire?" Piper asked. "Adler doesn't like to dance unless there lots of room for his wings. He once danced with my sister Blueberry and flew her a couple times into the air. She squealed. My biggest sister wants to go to the Bridal Faire but Da says no. They can meet young men at the local Fetes."

"I was not one of zhe young ladies at zhe festival. I sold fruit in a stall. Adler came every day to eat."

"I liked her more than the girls of the Faire," Adler added. "Plus many of them had scary mothers. No one talks about the scary mothers when they talk about the Faire."

"You could have taken your mom, Adler. She's scary. And she has claws on her feet," Piper said.

Ayperi looked at Adler.

"My mother is not scary. She doesn't like rowdiness, though. And of course she has claws on her feet. She's a Griffintaur. But normally she paints them pink."

"Trust me, Ayperi, they expected Adler to return with a real horror of a wife. They are all so jealous!" Piper. He waved a biscuit at Adler. "You were lucky to do so well without me to advise you."

"Well, I just kept thinking, would Piper like her? And Ayperi was the only one to pass the Piper test. Many of the girls seemed far too snooty."

That made Piper grin and others at the chuckle.

"PONDO, HARL, WOULD you join me in my office after supper? Master Shoji asked quietly. Adler and Mrs. Goldhawk will discuss the sorcerers they encountered on your journey. We will discuss security measures."

The four young people joined Master Shoji in his office.

"Adler and Ayperi had trouble with a group of sorcerers on their journey here. Ayperi, may I tell them about your past."

"Yes, Master."

"Ayperi was stolen from her home and sold at a slave market in the southern sea. She was purchased by an old woman named Changa and her son Lerg. They are sorcerers of dark magic. While Adler and Ayperi got away from the city safely, they were found on their journey by Lerg and two other sorcerers using a flying carpet. Adler and Ayperi managed to best them, destroying their carpet. From what Ayperi overheard with her time with Changa, they needed her for a purpose, and they needed her to stay a virgin. They told her she was a slave, and with no knowledge that Elvanor is a country where slavery is illegal, she stayed with Changa as a servant."

Harl lost his smirk. "Changa? A dark faun woman?"

"Yes."

"When I was small I had to have a guard because a hag named Changa was stealing small boys."

"Do you remember where you lived at that time?" Master Shoji asked.

"South. Southeast. Not in Cliffshire. We moved north when I was ten before I started school here."

"Very good, Harl. I will investigate." Master Shoji smiled. "So, extra patrols and a night watch in the fire tower. We do not think the sorcerers will know about the school but will head to Goldhawk Stronghold. I will send a missive on the wind tonight."

LORD MAGNUS GOLDHAWK Of Cliffshire
  Goldhawk Stronghold
  Dear Lord Goldhawk,
  I am writing to inform you that your son Adler arrived at the school earlier today, obediently wed. His bride, Ayperi, is a young

woman from the distant southern desert land of Zareemjarem. She is Sea Siren on her mother's side and Desert Fae royalty on her father's. She is lovely and well-mannered. They seem well suited to each other. Adler is anxious to get back to his studies, while Ayperi is working alongside my dear wife. Jeniski will provide Ayperi with education on Elvanor and woodwitch magic. Ayperi learned the magic of her family in her desert home, but it is different, being a land with no Glister.

You might receive a visit from the son of Ayperi's former employer, an unsavory wizard named Lerg, who tried to cause them trouble along the road. He may have knowledge of Adler's home from the magistrate who married the two. Since Adler and Ayperi were able to destroy Lerg's flying carpet, I doubt he will be of any real challenge for you and your men. Others were helping him, though, so be watchful. Adler says he smells of death and Ayperi says he and his mother do evil magic. His mother, Changa, might be a hag-faun from the southeast, perhaps Belvale Shire.

In light of this information, I am setting a watch at the school. If I feel we are under any threat I will ask for volunteer guards from our patrons.

Sincerely,

Anje Shoji

Headmaster

Glister Academy of Magicks

Master Shoji placed his pen back in the holder, folded the letter into a winged shape, and covered it with a dot of wind ointment which collected Glister sparkles. He opened the window and called a breeze to blow north to Goldhawk Stronghold. When the breeze arrived he released the correspondence to wisk away to Lord Goldhawk. He looked out the window of his high tower office, enjoying the sunset on the hills and mountains in the distance, the sweet fragrance of apple blossoms in the air.

Below, Adler and his bride walked in the apple orchards hand in hand, talking and laughing as they went. Adler tucked a spray of blossoms into her curls and Ayperi reached up to press a kiss on his lips.

Ah, young newlyweds!

A movement to the east, near the lilacs, caught his attention. A moment later the long full mane revealed it to be Harl, sneaking up on the newlyweds, probably to do some spying.

Master Shoji sighed. If anyone needed a good strong-minded bride, it was Harl. How many times had he bitten his tongue to keep from asking his wife to brew an anti-lust potion! One of these days a village maid would come to call, along with her father and every male relative, with weapons. If any of the boys need a wise wife, it was Harl. His youth in the military camps with all the whores and camp followers had given him a skewed view of women. Yet he wasn't a bad fellow.

Hmm. A wife for Harl? None of the snow fauns were quite old enough. There was poor, rejected Bufflindia, daughter of the Lesser Giant Chief Halgyr. The Halgyr females were known for their strong wills. And strong arms. The family was hardworking and moderately wealthy due to their mines and lovely jewelry talents. Harl would be lonely after Pondo married, and the new accommodations would have room for another married couple. He was a big fellow, a lesser giant bride would be a bit taller and wider, but not outlandishly so.

And Bufflindia with her long blond braids and deep dimples was quite fetching. He'd heard she was disappointed at the marriage contract denial by Adler's father, and had taken off for the Wildwood Mountains with a small mining cart. *A possibility?*

Master Shoji leaned out the window and amplified his voice with a charm. "Harl. Chop wood. Haul water."

Harl hung his head and gave a nod, and then ran off to chop and haul. Master Shoji waggled his head. Boys. Well, time to intervene. He pulled out another roll of parchment.

Dear Commander Valn,

I am writing to you about a possible marriage contract for your son Harl. I recently became aware that the Lesser Giant Chieftain Garfang Halgyr has an eligible daughter, Bufflindia. Her marriage contract recently fell through. Perhaps I can help you negotiate a new contract for your son Harl? Both his classmates will be wed for their final year at school, and I fear Harl will be lonely. Chieftain Halgyr has mines in his lands in the Wildwoods. They mine, make and sell fine jewelry. Bufflindia is quite a fine jeweler. Also, she has a strong objection to leaving the family Mountainhold. I suspect a warrior guard would be welcome in that family, due to transporting their fine jewelry to the Cities. Harl has talent as a battle mage.

I would be happy to write a letter of introduction to Chieftain Halgyr.

Sincerely,

Anje Shoji

Headmaster

Glister Academy of Magicks

Chapter Seven

They woke with the rooster crows just as the sun was turning the sky to gray. Breakfast was served quickly on napkins for easy cleanup. Families of the students began to show up with their carts pulled by horses or gnarlhogs. It was common for the families to caravan together to Goldhawk Stronghold. A good six hours on the road would see them there. The Stronghold would have a large buffet set up for the travelers coming to the Fest. The mood of the caravan was festive with lots of laughter.

Adler and Ayperi were taking the airboat. Harl and Piper were traveling with them, Piper because of incessant begging, and Harl for his excellent crossbow skills. Master Shoji didn't expect any trouble on the road, but it didn't hurt to be prepared. There had been no reports of strangers in the area of the festival from the Goldhawk Stronghold garrison. The festival marketplace would draw peddlers and merchants from all around the area and might be more of a risk. But the journey north from the school should be safe enough, and once they were at the Stronghold, only family could get into the castle built into the cliff.

The journey north was smooth, with no incidents. Adler warned people of large mud puddles. Several of the larger wagons had wooden planks they could put down to help others cross boggy areas. The caravan stopped briefly for a midday meal consisting of ale, crusty bread with cheese and dried apple tarts. Laughter and happy chatter filled the air.

In the early afternoon they came to a river valley. On the far side of the river, Ayperi saw a small village in front of a high golden cliff. The cliff gradually receded into a wood ridge, and she could see a mountain range far behind it, to the north.

"There it is, the gold stone cliffs. That is Goldhawk Stronghold. It was carved into the cliff side centuries ago," Adler said. As they got closer she could see high arched windows with balconies and towers on the top. "That's the Glint River which flowed through the village to the east and eventually joins the Searun and flows to the sea."

Soon she could see the Great Hall doors were open with a ramp over a moat o the village. Adler told her that individuals that couldn't fly to a balcony were helped into the building with a basket, pulley and rope system or took the inner staircases.

There was no bridge over the river but there were three ferries festooned with streamers to take wagons to the other side. Their camping area was in a broad meadow beyond the small village within easy walking distance of the festival grounds, on the Stronghold side of the river. Pavilions made of canvas adorned with flowers and bright flags and streamers were set up close to the village. Merchant stalls were busy. Music of pipes and drums drifted up from the grounds. Horses and gnarlhogs were already staked out or fenced on the far side in the broad meadow close to the river.

"I'm lowering the airboat to that balcony," Adler called, pointing to a wide, long balcony on the fourth level of the Stronghold. "I wasn't sure it would fit but it is small enough.

Watch your hands, you don't want to get scraped against the stone."

It took a few minutes to angle the airboat just right. "Harl, use the lead rope to tie it down while I set the anchors on the balcony and nullify the lifting elixir." Soon the airboat landed gently on the stone balcony and was secured to the stone railing. Piper clambered over the side while Adler lifted Ayperi out. Harl helped with the luggage. "These are my rooms. You two are going to meet your families in the Great Hall, yes?" Harl and Piper nodded. "I'm sure food is already set up for early arrivals in the Great Hall. Come, I'll show you the way."

They followed Adler from the balcony into a large sitting room filled with golden brown furniture with dark blue seat cushions. A huge fireplace filled one wall. It was far more opulent than the school.

"Nice place, Adler," Harl said, no sarcasm in his voice for a change. Ayperi wondered if Harl realized he would probably be working as a soldier for Adler one day. He didn't seem so arrogant now. In fact, he had been quiet the entire journey, scanning the road below and the skies for threats or problems. Not what she had expected.

"Heir apparent quarters. Got to move in when I turned eighteen. Before then, I had a room on the fifth floor. That's the children's floor." He waved at a stone stairway lit with magical lamps. "These stairs take you to the Great Hall, from there you go to the market since the ramp is down. I'm sure Mother sets out tons of food." Piper and Harl headed down.

"I'm sure we are expected to change into new clothes," Adler said to Ayperi after the students left. "Let me give you a tour. This is where we'll live after I finish school. We have a couple of houses on the land, also, but they are pretty isolated. After I am the Shire wizard I will need to be at the Stronghold so people can find me easily in an emergency. I will work defense charms with the garrison and make medical brews for the ill, charm things for people, especially winter fires. The people of the shire can come to the Stronghold for aid instead of purchasing in the market, if they want."

Through a set of double doors was another sitting room, this one with several tables with chairs and cushioned foot stools. It had a staircase to the fifth floor. "The Private Parlor, for just us or family. We can have meals in here." A hallway led to two empty bedrooms and a shared bath. "Extra room for guests or a nursery," Adler said. "There is a much larger nursery on the fifth floor, that's were the staircase leads."

He opened another door. "My Study." It held a desk and a bookshelf full of books. "The Stronghold has an enormous still room that will be one of my responsibilities. I have a large private workroom near it, where I will probably spend most of my time."

"Is your father a wizard also? It seems to be a big job."

"No, my father trained as a soldier. He was in the King's Guard. We hired a Shire wizard. His name is Jolan, from the land of Emrysdell. He was a student with Master Shoji. In a few years he hopes to retire and move back to his village in Emrysdell."

"This is our room." The bed was huge and had gold velvet curtains. Adler opened the curtain at the foot of the bed. "The moonlight floods in."

He grinned and she found herself blushing. He was certainly bolder than he had been when they first married. She liked that about him. The large window facing south had a door that opened to a small balcony large enough for a few chairs and a table. Attached to the bedroom was a bathing area with a toilet that similar to what they had at the school. The bath, however, was huge, more like a pool in the floor, made of smooth blue tile.

In the bedroom there was a small seating area near the fireplace and a writing desk. Another door led to a sunny room. "Your study. My mother uses hers for reading racy books bought from the lesser giants."

"I will continue to study to learn Elvanor ways. I will put it to good use."

"Let's find clothes." The bedroom held two large wardrobes against one wall. "I vonder if the clothing your mother had made for us is in them." Ayperi opened one and gasped at the variety of gowns. Floral day dresses, thin pastel linens, several silk gowns, and one eggshell lace and silk creation embroidered in pastel flowers, extremely formal, with a train.

"That is what you will wear tonight at the Marriage Blessing." Adler's mother planned a marriage blessing ceremony at the Midsummer Night Feast instead of a complete marriage ceremony. She had sent letters with their speaking parts so Ayperi would be comfortable with the ceremony.

There was a knock on Adler's bedroom door. Adler opened the door to a small brown faun woman with a big grin.

"Hi Misty, how are your kids?" Adler gave her a big hug.

The woman giggled. "They are with their father and uncles while I am here helping your mother today. Thank the Green Lady. All are wild with excitement."

"I'll look for them at the Feast." Adler took Ayperi's hand. "Misty, my wife Ayperi."

Misty grabbed her hands and squeezed them, smiling warmly. "How lovely you are! Let me help you find a day dress. I fear Lady Mirilia went overboard with the seamstress." She turned to Adler. "You should wear the dark blue trimmed with blue velvet. Or the golden brown broadcloth. You had best wait until milady picks her gown. Your mother wouldn't want you to clash," she said.

"Oh, the horror."Adler nodded and went to the other wardrobe. There was a dressing screen next to each wardrobe.

"Come, Lady Ayperi, we will choose a day dress."

Ayperi soon found herself wearing a pale blue dress with mid-length sleeves with flounces of eyelet and a square neckline, also trimmed in eyelet. The bodice was soft white leather with blue and pink floral embroidery and blue ribbons. The gown was very lightweight and reached just above her ankles. Underneath she wore an eyelet petticoat and pantaloons trimmed in eyelet. Several sizes of white leather slippers were in the wardrobe, as well as soft white stockings.

"Tonight you will wear the eggshell gown for the feast. It is lovely. You will look perfect in it! You will be introduced as Adler's bride, of course."

Adler wisely put on the blue coat, white shirt, and trousers, which buttoned below his knees. Ayperi grinned at him. Adler generally wore the plainest of work clothes, often stained by potions. Now he looked like a hero in one of her mother's romance songs.

"Your parents are in the Gold Parlor. With everyone," Millie winked.

The Gold Parlor was enormous and filled with women seated on gold velvet couches and chairs. "Any female relative or elderly woman of the Shire with no family to care for them is welcome here," Adler murmured into her ear. "There is a similar group of men, but they lodge in the garrison quarters on the north side of the Stronghold."

Small tables and chairs, couches, seating areas, and a long buffet table filled the room. The walls were striped with shiny gold paint and Ayperi wondered if it was real gold. Women, mostly griffintaurs, filled the room. She saw a few small children. Most were elderly but she saw a few younger women. She noticed an elderly faun woman in a tiny wheelchair which seemed to be propelled by magic. She saw sparks of Glister around the wheels.

A tall blond Griffintaur woman wearing a yellow lace gown sat in a fine chair near the balcony. The man who sat next to her in the matching chair wore tan and gold. His hair was shaved short around the ears but on top, it was a mass of unruly curls, more gray than gold.

"Mother, Father, let me introduce my bride, Ayperi of Oleander Oasis, Zareemjarem."

His mother flew out of her chair and Ayperi's saw her wings were more white than gold. She embraced Adler and then turned to Ayperi. "I have heard good things about you from Madam Shoji." Then she embraced Ayperi. "Poor child, so far from home. You must consider us your family now. I am so pleased Adler chose so well, I truly expected one of those spoiled miniature flying pony girls that are all the rage."

Adler snorted. "I did not even speak to one of them the entire Bridal Faire."

Lady Goldhawk smiled a knowing smile. "No doubt you spent more time playing Rockroll with other young men. Nevertheless, I believe good fortune found you."

Lord Goldhawk was a bit taller than Adler and much wider, with heavily muscled arms. He wore a dagger with a jeweled handle in a belt which also held a long thin sword."Welcome child!" Lord Goldhawk embraced her and then directed them to a table on the balcony where a buffet meal had been placed. "Come, let us get to know each other. I'm sure you are hungry."

"The gown suits you. I confess I wrote Mistress Shoji to find out what you looked like," Mirilia said. "I had never heard of Coral Sea Sirens before, but your hair is stunning." They reached the table which held various small meat pies, biscuits with butter and jam, fruit cakes and small baked potatoes and stuffed mushrooms. All food meant to be eaten easily in this informal setting. Others followed after them in line, filling porcelain platters with nice rims around the edges to keep food from falling as they moved about the room.

"My sisters," Adler walked with her to a seating area near his parent's chairs. "Fortuna is my older sister," He indicated a tall, big-boned woman who looked a great deal like his mother. "Married to Hradgreave of Garth Shire to our east." Hradgreave was a griffintaur with white hair and wings, though he was not much older than Adler.

"Their daughter Tilia."

The child had a merry smile. "I'm eight!" Tilia informed her.

"Eight is a wonderful age, " Ayperi grinned back at the little girl with long, butter yellow ringlets.

"Abundia, my second sister. She is the mother of these two rascals, Garth and Heath, the twin terrors. They are four. She lives here in Cliffshire, with her husband Captain Megol." Abundia was smaller than her sister with caramel brown hair and startling blue eyes. Her husband had dark brown wings with gold tips to his dark feathers and dark brown hair streaked with gold. The twins had brown curls and bright blue eyes. They squirmed around and seemed eager to get out of the room.

Ayperi and Adler walked around the room meeting the many female dependents that lived in the castle. Some were widows, some were spinsters and most were quite elderly. A few were lame or had other disabilities and needed care. All were dressed well in light day dresses. She also met the older gentlemen, wearing their best suits. Some were former soldiers or men so elderly they had outlived family. Adler treated them all as family, which warmed her heart. All of them were very interested in the airboat.

After wandering for some time they rejoined Adler's parents, sitting together on a small couch. "Before we go back to the school perhaps we can take the airboat out to Blue Loon Lake for a picnic. We can make several trips, take the ladies and gents," Adler said.

"Wonderful idea, I will get the kitchen to add a picnic to the menu," Lady Goldhawk said. "Ayperi, do you swim? If it is warm we can swim in the lake."

"Yes. I swam the sea with my muzzer and the Oasis with my Fazzer. We often played on the beach as children and mother insisted we know how to swim."

"I will have the seamstress fix you a bathing dress. I have several brand-new ones, we'll just need to get one fitted."

"Ayperi, tell us about your family," Lord Goldhawk requested. "Your father is an Oleander Oasis fairy, what is that? Master Shoji will consult our Mage Jolan about a way yo send your parents a message."

"My fazzer is a Fae Prince and his oasis is called zhe Oleander Oasis. Zhere are rivers in the desert but most of zhem dry up in the summer. 'Tis very hot. But zhe desert is dotted with Oases. Zhey are beautiful green places vith deep pools, and zhe pools are magical. Zhe Desert Fae control zhe waters. Sending streams to farms and orchards after zhe rivers and brooks dry. It is magic only zhey can do, and all zhe farms and orchards would die without zhe fae. Every pool is in a place with great magical power, a sanctuary for all people and beings of beings. My fazzer makes sure zhe Oleander Oasis remains free for all people across the desert, otherwise greedy strongmen will hold the Oases and many will suffer. Zhe Desert Fae believe the water of the desert needs to be free."

"And your mother lives on the coast, they are not living together?"

"Zhe Desert Fae can only marry other Fae, so their children call zhe waters. My sisters and I cannot call water. Perhaps when we are older, but it is not an early power. He has an heir, his sister's son, Taavi. His family is kind to us and to my muzzer. My mozzer has the siren voice and gets too lonely for zhe sea at the Oasis. She must refresh in the sea with her sisters. We children traveled between."

"And do you sing?"

"No, I am not a singer. My oldest sister Kiralla has zhe singing talent and is bound to zhe sea, like my mozzer. My sister Zuhanna is a little older zhan me, we have not found our talent yet. We are not old enough to have our powers but singers have zheir voice early. My little sister Adrina is too young for any talents or powers yet."

"Some in her family have far-seeing powers and far-moving powers. I suspect that is why the evil wizard wanted her, in the hopes of exploiting her talent," Adler said.

"Well, that's interesting. Perhaps Master Shoji and our wizard can try to get a message on the winds to Ayperi's parents." Mirilia smiled at them. "But now I think all the young people would enjoy some time at the festival. Dinner will not be until eight at night, with the Blessing right before the meal. After the meal, we will have a bonfire with the midsummer moon ritual. I will have a servant remind you to come back and dress for dinner. Did you see the gown, Ayperi? You will look lovely."

"What about security, Father? I told you about the evil wizard that is interested in my wife."

"I have hired a small band of orcs from Hobb. They are on the roads and paths leading to town. The garrison and staff are aware they had a flying carpet. I have watchmen on the towers."

THEY WANDERED THE FESTIVAL grounds and collected a number of children companions. Tilia walked next to Ayperi, chatting about everything. Soon Fortuna, Abundia and her little boys joined them. Piper, Marcil and Piper's thirteen-year-old twin sisters, Pinkberry and Lilacberry, joined them as well

"I see Rockroll is already drawing a crowd."

"There is Grunhilda," Abundia said, pointing to a giantess in a red floral gown with a red leather bodice.

Adler waved at the giantess who grinned at him and held a round rock ball as large as her head. "Later," he called to her. "I don't see Bufflindia," he said. She was usually with her mother.

Fortuna and Abundia shared a glance. "Well, Bufflindia was a bit upset about the contract not being signed."

"What?" Adler looked astonished. "Really? I can't believe Bufflindia had any deep feelings for me. She mostly just wanted to beat me in Rockroll. And last Midsummer she was kissing a centaur with long blond hair. Behind a booth, where her mother couldn't see."

"I don't think it was your contract so much as the several contracts her family received right after Father didn't sign yours," Fortuna said. "Bufflindia refuses to move to Jorghenbag and marry a merchant."

Abundia nodded, eyes huge."She took her brother Gordo's clothes and boots, hitched up a mining wagon and headed out into the mountains one night."

"She left a letter for her father. Any man who wanted her to marry would have to find her in the wildwood." Fortuna took over the story. Ayperi grinned in amusement at how the two switched off the telling.

"They haven't found her?"

"No. The family received a message on the wind that she would not be at the festival, she was busy mining, making her own fortune."

"Also, if any man had the woodcraft to find her, she would give half her cache of jewels as additional dowry. And that her mine was profitable."

"Now her father is negotiating a contract with a student from your school. A Horsetail faun. Battle magics."

"Oh, Harl." Piper snorted. "Harl and Bufflindia? I just don't see it," Piper said. "He is the only battle mage student at the school. You should see him conjure a sword! And he is as tall as Adler."

"Harl is so handsome," Pinkberry said. Her sister nodded."He wears his hair shaved in the sides so it looks like a mane."

"Redberry says we must stay away from him," Lilacberry said with a pout.

"I agree with that!" Adler said and Piper nodded.

"He has no manners," Piper said.

Abundia laughed. "Bufflindia will soon take care of that!"

"I can't even imagine Harl with a wife. But then, until Father sent me to the Faire, I couldn't imagine myself with a wife, either." He kissed Ayperi on the cheek.

Chapter Eight

"We got up awfully early this morning. I think I could use a little nap. Perhaps we should retire to our quarters for a little nap?"Adler whispered in Ayperi's ear as they walked along.

"Zhat is a great idea. I've had enough sun and mead for now." Giggling like children hiding from a schoolmate they walked quickly away from their companions who were busy with a game booth. Adler pulled her into a narrow space between two booths, a rolled up canvas wall hiding them from the thoroughfare. She smelled like honeysuckle and affected his brain like too much honey mead. His lips crushed hers in a searing kiss, his tongue plundering her sweet mouth, his entire body shivering with lightning thrills as her tongue greeted his with equal hunger.

It would be faster to fly her to his room. But people would see. Her hand slid down his chest as they remained latched at the mouth. A hot little hand yanked up his tunic and planted itself on his middle, sliding up over his nipples, which sent a shock through him. Until this month with her in his bed, he never even knew a man's nipples could feel so good.

His legs tremble. He wanted those hands to slide down so bad, into his breeches.

"Oh. Up. Fly." He had lost the ability to speak.

He dragged her out to the walkway and launched up into the air. She squealed and wrapped her arms about his neck, soon followed by her legs around his hips. He no longer cared if the old ladies were giggling at them. Adler went straight to his bedroom balcony. He tossed her on the bed and rushed to his baggage and pulled out a wicker charm which he hung on the key that locked his doors to the stairs. Turning back to her he whipped off his tunic, hearing the tie around his neck snap.

"Privacy charm."

Ayperi's lips curved in a knowing smirk. "What about the balcony? Couldn't someone fly through there?"

"No. Special charm. The stone carvings." He sounded like a mangled brain idiot.

"Excellent." Ayperi rose onto her knees, unlacing her leather bodice as her hips swayed, then tossing it on the table next to the bed. She kicked her shoes off. Adler was just standing there staring at her. "Oh, do you want to watch me, husband?" She grinned and pulled the gown over her head. Underneath the gown, she wore a sheer shift edged with lace and embroidery, very pretty. "A gift from Mistress Shoji. Eye catching!" Looking him straight in the eyes she slowly pulled off the thin shift. Her knickers were also of the same sheer fabric. "My stockings are attached to my pantalets. I have to untie the ribbons." She slid off the bed and bent over, tilting her cream bottom, just barely visible through the thin fabric. Adler groaned and with a flap of his wings, he landed on his knees on the bed behind her. His hands cupped the round globes. He pressed an open mouth kiss on one plump cheek, open mouth, his tongue feeling the texture of the cloth. Ayperi untied the garter and slid the stockings down her legs wiggling just so.

She giggled at the sound of his raspy voice. "You need to catch up, Adler. Let's get those clothes off." She climbed onto the bed and started to untie his jacket and thin shirt.

Adler was so excited he couldn't speak. They had waited so long for this. He had seen her naked in firelight and candlelight many times but today seeing her in the strong sunlight in his rooms in the castle was somehow more intense. Her skin, so creamy and soft, and her hair picked up lights from the sun and glittered almost like Glister. Like she herself was magic. He put that thought away for later. Nipples rose high and called to him. He lifted her and then placed her on the pillowy bed, his mouth finding the hard tip of a nipple. It thrilled him that she was aroused by him. Her hands threaded through his hair, making him shiver. Who knew fingers in his hair would feel so sexy. Thrills through him landed in his cock, his tip was already seeping.

Her skin was flushed to the rounded curves of her breasts, her lips dark red and parted in anticipation of more hard, hungry kisses. He ground himself against her thigh and then groaned. That was a mistake if he actually wanted to get inside her and come.

He slid down her, planting kisses on that firm belly. She smelled intoxicating. He wiggled his shoulder between her legs, and she arched her back. "Yesss."

He breathed on the nearly purple curls at her juncture. So perfect, those plump lips, the sheen of her desire had him panting for a taste. She tasted like nothing he had ever imagined, salty, tangy sweet.

His tongue found her sweet button, and he sucked and licked with vigor, knowing he couldn't wait much longer. "Sweetheart," he whispered. "My bride."

And then her legs were around his shoulders he could feel her little feet on his wings and that was a delightful sensation. Her hands gripped his hair as he worked the sweet wet pool between her legs. She moaned and gripped his hair over and over again. "In me now," she said. "Now."

He knew she had not reached her peak but who was he to argue. She was begging him to do what he most wanted to do. He pressed his aching, wet cock between her legs. She lifted her legs up and wrapped them around his hips. "I don't want to hurt you," he whispered.

"Do it," she countered. "It will be alright," she breathed. "Potion helps."

Adler found her sweet well and slid into her. His breath was hard. "You can move," she whispered into his neck, her tongue leaving a trail.

"No control," He gasped. He moved a little, so he was along her side, not crushing her with his weight. She grabbed his hand and wiggled it between them. He knew what she wanted and one finger found her plump button. Then he could feel her gripping his cock with her inner muscles. No one had told him women could do that. "Amazing" he groaned. He realized she had just come and then so did he like a lightning flash. Behind his eyes he saw white hot sparkles. Magic.

When he could think again he was lying half on top of her, sweaty, still breathing hard. He moved, and she shifted, so she was half on top of him. "Perhaps it's too soon to say but I think

I will soon love you," he whispered. "Do you think it happens so quickly?"

"I think it can. I think I will soon love you too. Or maybe I do already."

Adler pressed a soft kiss to her swollen lips. "Maybe I do too."

THE MARRIAGE BLESSING was mercifully short. Ayperi knew the dress was lovely but standing in front of a huge crowd was frightening. All the eyes upon her, the strange woman from far away. Adler held both of her hands in his, and constantly caressed the backs of her hands with his thumbs. At least all they had to do was confirm their marriage. They stood in front of Lord Goldhawk, resplendent in grass green robes.

"I, Ayperi of Oleander Oasis and the Coral Sea Siren Clan of Zareemjarem am wife to Adler by choice and magic."

"I, Adler Goldhawk, Heir Apparent to the Karl of Cliffshire, am husband to Ayperi by choice and magic."

"May this marriage be blessed with a meeting of hearts. As our land flourishes, so may this husband and wife. So mote it be."

Hundreds of celebrants, many who had far too much to drink, repeated the phrase, and then cheered and clapped. She was so relieved when they were guided to the Head Table for the Midsummer Feast. Following the Feast was the Midsummer Fire.

"We all gather round," intoned Lord Goldhawk. People circled a large firepit. "May our crops grow with vigor and bring us abundant Harvest. May our people be strong and wise. May our beasts feed and grow strong. May our rivers, lakes, wells and pools hold clear water. May we, the people of Cliffshire prosper, as we honor the old ways and the gods of the Circle. Now is the time to come forth with your offerings and requests."

He took a sheaf of braided wheat from the previous harvest covered with spring flowers and threw it into the pit then to his left his wife get the same but hers was a rolled-up scroll. Each person, as their time came, tossed something into the fire. Food, flowers, an item of clothing or a scroll tied with ribbon.

Ayperi saw that soon her turn would come. "Adler what are they doing? I have nothing to give."

"I have something, a small scroll tied with flowers." He brought it out of his pocket. "To bless our marriage and a promise help each other be strong together. We can give it together has a married couple. If you want. Or I can give it myself, for the two of us."

" All right." When their turn came they held small scroll and walked forward hand in hand, tossing it into the fire. Glister danced above the fire, their offering joining their neighbors.

When every person had had their turn at the fire pit all the people joined hands in the circle and raised them above their heads. "So mote it be," said Lord Goldhawk.

The people echoed him, "So mote it be." Glister twinkled above the fire and spread away, to all corners of the land.

After it left the fire pit vendors returned to their booths. Rockroll players headed toward the lanes, Children ran for the games and treats, while adults lined up at the ale and mead kegs. Ayperi and Adler wandered the fairway, people greeting them wherever they went. It wasn't long before the group of children they'd had as companions earlier in the day joined them again. Ayperi played some games and learned to do a circle dance with Adler. It was fun even though she didn't know the steps, with Adler flying her into her up into the sky and back down to the ground. She giggled constantly, and she and Adler stole a kiss now and then

They came to the Rockroll Lanes, and she persuaded Adler to play a few games. She knew he loved and tried to learn the intricacies of the Rockroll.

It was hours after midnight, she was sure. The pan pipes and drums played quick lively tunes, the griffintaur dancers were doing more and more air based dance steps, lofting and swooping in a way that made her stomach feel odd. The festival only grew in intensity as the night wore on. She suspected it would run until dawn. Ayperi had never had so much to drink in her life. Wine with lunch. Ale on the Festival grounds. Wine and mead with dinner. Fruit punch made with wine and kept cold with chunks of ice, something she had not seen in her homelands. More ale at the Rockroll lanes.

She needed water.

Adler's young nieces and nephews had commandeered her for a few minutes to admire their dance. "Zhat was a lovely dance. Why don't we find something to drink? I would like water or juice."

"They are refreshments at the pavilion. And pies and tarts!" The children wanted sweets. "Butter brickle, too!" Piper was enthusiastic about sweets. She let Adler know they were going to the pavilion for treats.

The children were a bit loud, having sampled more ale than they should since their parents had let them roam the Fairgrounds without much supervision. They dragged Piper along when he got into an ale line. "I think not, my friend." He just grinned.

The head table was empty of people now, everyone was on the Festival grounds. The children swarmed the desserts. Ayperi found a refreshing mug of water with strawberries floating in it. She sat at the table, tired from the long day and so much activity. The children found jugs of milk in the icebox and had a feast of sweets.

The people she could see were raucous. Many were inebriated. Security...it seemed rather lax. How easy would it be for Lerg to slide through the crowd? She shivered. Surely they had some type of protection she was unaware of. She'd met the elderly head wizard, Jolan. He did not seem a fool.

It probably wasn't best to be isolated, though. Luckily she was surrounded by half a dozen children, including Piper and his twin sisters, her griffintaur niece Tilia, a few of the younger boys from school, and a small Black Dwarf boy named Glarg who would join the Academy next year. When they were finally finished devouring the sweets Ayperi said, "I should go find Adler. He is playing Rockroll still, I am sure."

"We'll go with you. Bufflindia has a new suitor, so her mother is teaching him to roll rock since Bufflindia refused to come to the Festival." Tilia giggled. "We want to see him. He is *so* handsome."

Piper groaned. "He's Harl. Truly not that handsome once you get to know him. Kind of grumpy. And rude."

"Well, I'm not going to marry him. I'm just going to look at him," The twins giggled. "My mom says Bufflindia can handle him."

The children argued Harl's appearance and personality while they walked through the loud crowds back toward the Rockroll lanes. They all agreed Bufflindia would teach him manners.

Moving through the center of the festival grounds was too slow due to the crowd, so they moved to the outskirts of the crowd where they could walk more freely. Something flashed past Ayperi's vision, and then she felt a rope yank around her waist and arms pulling her into the air. The rope was invisible. She screamed and looked up to see a flying carpet, nearly transparent in the night sky. *Bespelled.*

Chapter Nine

"Tell Adler that Lerg has me! Flying carpet with invisible charms! Go, go now!" The children took off in a burst of speed, except for little Tilia. She instead took to the air and followed.

"I can barely see you, Aunt Ayperi! I will try to follow you."

"No! These men are horrible. It is too dangerous. Go find Adler!"

But the child had a determined look on her face and continued to fly after her. The men on the carpet weren't shooting bolts at the child.

They don't want to be seen. Shooting bolts of energy at Tilia would give away their location.

Tilia put two fingers in her mouth and gave a high-pitched, very loud whistle. She did it over and over.

They were soon flying near the tower guards on the towers of the Stronghold. Ayperi screamed at them. Tilia whistled.

"Shut that kid up!" Someone on the carpet yelled.

"No! We don't want to attract any notice." That was Changa screeching.

The charmed rope tightened and yanked her toward the carpet, but when it did it caused the carpet to dip and list.

"Leave her hanging." Lerg's rough voice yelled to the others on the carpet. "We'll land soon enough. The pursuers will not catch what they can't see."

Ayperi could still see the Festival grounds, and she saw Griffintaurs take to the air. Adler would come for her. *Her strong, beautiful husband, would she ever—* No! She would not consider that their life together was over, ended by these evil men. Their marriage had been blessed by magic. They loved each other. Even if they were too afraid to admit it, yet.

"When we can, we'll swoop down and get that flyer girl. She'll sell for much gold. People at the slave market have never even heard of griffintaurs!" One of the evil ones shouted.

Tilia began to tire, her flight becoming erratic.

"Tilia, land!"

"No, I am not leaving you." With a burst of effort, the child flew closer and closer to Ayperi. Finally, she was close, though Ayperi could move her arms to hold the child.

"Hang onto me, put your arms and legs about me." Ayperi instructed.

Tilia did so. "Aunt Ayperi, I have a dagger in my bodice. I'll try to cut the rope. Maybe I can fly you down."

The child barely weighed anything, as far as Ayperi could tell. "I think I will be too heavy for you. Just rest for now."

"Where did that griffintaur girl go?"

One of the sorcerers laughed. "She probably crashed."

"They can't see you here with me. They probably can't see me well, either, due to their charm. It covers us like a fog. Maybe that will help us escape," Ayperi whispered.

They were past the Stronghold now, in a farm area.

The Glister mocked her. From her aerial view, Ayperi could see pockets of it everywhere, in the fields, in stands of trees, in farmyards. If only she knew how to use it.

The carpet continued to move away from the Stronghold.

Ayperi felt something. Something familiar. A flash, a vision of Oleander Oasis... Graceful palm trees, the orchards... The fine, white-columned villa her father lived in.

The cool, deep blue water of the Oasis, giving life and beauty to the desert.

"Tilia, is there water near us? I can only see the Stronghold and a bit of the Festival Grounds."

"Yes. We are coming to Blue Lune Lake."

"Let's try and turn, so I can see the lake."

With some flaps of Tilia's wings and twisting they were able to see the lake. It was huge. Bordered by tall pine trees to the north and a wide shore to the south.

"Tilia, can you use your knife on the rope? It might be charmed, so maybe it can't be cut. Can you swim?"

"I can swim." Tilia got her knife out and started on the rope binding Ayperi's arms to her side. "Auntie, it cuts just like rope, but it's thick."

"That's alright. We are not yet over the lake. When we get there, we'll just drop and then swim to shore." *I hope.* She saw an occasional glimpse of wing in the distance.

Ayper's hands tingled. She wiggled her fingers, thinking it was the tight rope causing her hands to go numb. With work, she got her arms loose, scraping them on the rope. Water rippled in the lake, and stopped when she quit wiggling her fingers. *Am I doing that? Am I calling the waters?*

She swept her hand back and forth and waves followed. "Tilia. Maybe I can pull up a gentle wave of water that will sweep us down to the shore. It will be much safer than dropping into the center of the lake."

"All right. I'm almost done with the rope. Hold on."

Ayperi held on to the rop e above her. She felt the snap of the cut rope and grabbed it in her hands to hold on. Tilia flapped her wings and edged up, so she could hold the rope.

"We're almost over the lake. I'm going to try and call a wave to float us to the shore."

Tilia held onto the rope with both hands. Ayperi let go of the rope with one hand and waved it toward the lake. She whispered, "Gentle, gentle water, carry us to shore." In her mind, she visualized a wave reaching them and carrying them on its surface to the shore. She wasn't sure that was how water calling worked, but intention was all, wasn't it? "Allow the child and I to wash gently to shore."

A wave formed and grew larger and larger. Taller. It reached to the sky. Above her the sorcerers screamed and shot lightning bolts into the water, which only made the water steam. A moment later, a splash of icy water enveloped them, and they let go of the rope. Ayperi hung onto the child, not wanting her to be swept away from her. The water pushed them to the surface and then rushed them down to the lake, floating them across the surface to the sandy shore.

"Are you all right ? Ayperi screamed, terrified Tilia was hurt or worse.

"Cold," Tilia replied. Ayperi gathered the child into her arms. Above her, the carpet was bearing down on them. "Tilia, find a place to hide, they still have the carpet. I'm going to try to bring it down with the waters."

Tilia ran off to some tall grass and hid. Ayperi waded into the lake and held her hands upon the surface. She pictured a strong rush of water, like a whale's spout, only larger. "I ask you to keep us safe. Take down the carpet vit the evil sorcerers."

Cupping her hands, she flung water up toward the carpet with all her strength. A huge wave followed her movements and rushed upward, hitting the carpet with force, turning it end over end.

She heard Changa screeching in anger. "Grab them and toss them in the middle of the lake far from shore! Far from me, far from the child."

The wave swallowed the carpet and riders and rushed like a river toward the far side of the lake.

Frozen from the cold water, Ayperi crawled to the sand. "Tilia, are you there?"

"I'm here." Tilia came out looking sodden and miserable with cold. They met and Ayperi held her tight. They huddled together on the shore. "I'm sure we'll see someone soon."

"I can do my whistle. Griffintaurs ears can hear it from far away." Tilia blew her whistle.

It wasn't long before they could hear the flapping of wings. "Here!" Ayperi called. Adler landed next to her and pulled both of them into his arms.

"Th-The sorcerers are somewhere in the lake." His arms felt so good.

"The airboat is on its way. Until then, I will start a fire." Soon he had firerocks ablaze, and they scooted next to it, soaking in the heat.

A large group of griffintaurs flew overhead, with swords drawn and arrows notched."The garrison will take care of the sorcerers, if any are alive. How did you get them into the lake?"

"I called the water. I could feel it. So I had it take Tilia and me gently to shore, but I had it slam a wave into the carpet."

Epilogue

"**I** was a real idiot," Adler confessed into the ear of his bride. He glided the sponge gently over her shoulder, squeezing steaming water onto her exposed flesh.

"For letting me walk zhe Festival grounds with just children, late at night, surrounded by drunk people?"

The sponge paused. Adler took a quick breath. "Well, that too. I thought we had security taken care of. I guess none of us thought of invisible flying carpets."

Ayperi wiggled in her husband's lap. The airboat, with charmed blankets, had deposited her back at his rooms. They were greeted by a steaming, petal filled bath, and a hot sweet whiskey drink with cream to warm her from the inside.

"No one expected such a zhing." She trailed a finger down one thigh curved around her in the large bath.

"Uh, what I was talking about, the stupid thing... was when I said I might soon be in love with you. I was wrong to say that." His hand found her chin, and he turned her head a bit, so she could see him. "I do love you. Now. I loved you then, too. Except I was an idiot."

She turned and wrapped her arms around his neck. "I was an idiot, as well. While Tilia and I were in danger...I refused to zhink, to believe, I would never see you again. I knew I loved you, and that you loved me." She kissed him.

A FEW DAYS LATER ADLER, Ayperi and the other students gathered in the morning sun for their journey back to the school.

"I will not be returning to the school with you, Adler." Harl stood by the airboat wearing leathers, accompanied by a gnarlhog hauling a sizable pack.

"Looks like you are going on a rough journey." Adler scratched the gnarlhog's huge snout. "Fine beast you have here. Always liked a good gnarlhog." It was up to his chest and probably weighed three times his weight. Its tusks were half the length of Adler's arm.

"His name is Spot. I am off to the Wildwood west of Chieftain Halgyr's estate. My father and Chieftain Halgyr signed a marriage contract. I am to hike through the Wildwood and find my errant bride to be." He shrugged. "The gnarlhog and the gear are a gift from the Chieftain and his Lady."

"Bufflindia is a good woman. Tough and funny."

"Also far above my station. A chieftain's daughter marrying a common soldier! I guess I have you to thank for that. She could easily have married you."

Ayperi was walking to the airboat with his parents, little Tilia holding her hand. She smiled at him, flashing dimples. Her pink hair glowed in the morning sunshine.

"It worked out the way it was supposed to, Harl. Ayperi and I were meant for each other." Adler stuck out his hand. "A battle mage in the family makes sense for a family of jewelers. Good journey, Harl. Tell Bufflindia hello from me."

"I will." Harl nodded to Ayperi and Adler's parents and headed toward the river path.

His wife reached him, and he leaned down for a kiss. "Ready to go?"

"Yes. It has been a lovely visit, but I look forward to being back at home." Piper and his Dwarf friend Glarg, who was joining them for the final two weeks of school before summer break, clambered into the basket. "Ayperi, one of Adler's aunts gave us a whole basket of sweet tarts for the journey!"

"Lovely."

"Son, I heard from the Commander of the King's Guard," Lord Goldhawk said. "Lerg and his group of sorcerers are known to them. Their goal is to assassinate the king. To try to get one of their own on the throne. I've sent them down river with the garrison. The King will deal with them now."

"Zhey must have hoped I had zhe far-reaching talents. Much evil can be done from afar," Ayperi said.

Lord Goldhawk chuckled. "There is also much power in being able to throw half a lake at someone. I'm glad you have inherited your father's powers. Ayperi."

"Zhank you." After hugging her new family goodbye, Adler lifted her into the airboat.

"Good journey!" Adler's family called to them as they floated away.

A FEW WEEKS BEFORE Midwinter

Ayperi's hands shook as she received the scroll from Master Shoji.

"It came by ship to Norport and then by King's Messenger to me. It seems your father did receive our message." Last summer, Master Shoji, Adler and Jolan had combined magic to send a message on the wind to her father.

She unrolled the scroll. The flowing script of Zareemjarem seemed almost foreign after studying the more blocky script of the Norlands.

My Darling Daughter,

How we have missed you and longed to hear from you. We feared for your safety and very life, but the midwinter ritual assured us you were alive, and by some miracle, well. Your letter brought great rejoicing to all of Oleander Oasis and all your other family and friends.

We are well. After your abduction, I moved all your sisters to the Oasis, where security is much higher. Your mother was torn because she needed to sing and oversee her inn. Your Grandmother the Queen was quite upset. She gifted a team of her own winged gazelles, so your mother can live at the Oasis but travel to the inn to sing. We hired a half-Fae, half -faun gentleman to oversee the inn when she is here at the Oasis. His name is Tannus Sandhill. This fall he and Kirilla wed and are now expecting a child. I do worry about her safety in the city, but since she is a known Siren Singer and will never develop the far-reaching talents, slavers are less interested in her. She has a team of all female guards of great martial skill, from the Land Unwyn.

Your mother hopes to come visit you in Norland. As you know, I am bound to the Oasis and cannot leave, though I long to see you. I am trying to find a safe way for your mother and unmarried sisters to visit. The Queen may be able to unleash me from the Oasis, if my Heir can do the work of the Oasis. It would only be for a season, so I couldn't stay long in the north.

If possible, could I learn the method of messages on the wind? I know you have Glister magic, and we do not, but the Oasis is a powerful magical place. Perhaps I can adapt the method.

Please greet your husband, his family, and your Headmaster and his wife in my name. I owe you and all of them a debt for your safety.

I am thrilled you have the power to call the waters. It is rare for a half fae to have such.

Your sister Zuhanna has a magical way with potions. I think it might be related in away to water powers. Perhaps someday we will study this in depth.

All your family sends their love.
With my heart,
Your Father
Prince Zahur
Oleader Oasis
Zareemjarem

About The Author

BIO

Take a bookworm. Hand her a stack of, sci-fi and fantasy novels, thrillers and horror comics. Then introduce the world of romance.

Make her a jinx. Every great genre TV show she loves gets the ax! She gets upset about no romance in the world and writes her own stories with happy endings.

Throw this all together, shake constantly, and pour onto a computer keyboard.

There!

You have me, Melisse Aires.

Find me!

I have a newsletter! sendfox.com/melisseaires[1]
I can always be found on Facebook. I run the fun Scifi Romance Group[2] and also Romancing the Shire[3]. My personal group is Melisse Aires' Lair[4]

BLOG: https://melisseaireswriter.wordpress.com/
Website:
http://www.melisseairesbooks.weebly.com[5]
Facebook: https://www.facebook.com/melisseaires
IO News Group:https://groups.io/g/MelisseAiresPureEscapism

---

1. http://sendfox.com/melisseaires

2. https://www.facebook.com/groups/the.scifi.romance.group/

3. https://www.facebook.com/groups/romancingtheshire/

4. https://www.facebook.com/groups/1732565730395151

5. http://www.melisseairesbooks.com

Please review if you enjoyed this romance!

Don't miss out!

Visit the website below and you can sign up to receive emails whenever Melisse Aires publishes a new book. There's no charge and no obligation.

https://books2read.com/r/B-A-PTK-LYPZ

BOOKS 2 READ

Connecting independent readers to independent writers.

Also by Melisse Aires

Another Supernatural Apocalypse
Enchanted Bonds
Ritual of Fire and Ice

A Warm Winter Fantasy
Elf Wish
Christmas Wizardry
Faunication

Cyborg Nation
A Cyborg's Old Terran Christmas

Diaspora Worlds
Her Cyborg Awakes
Alien Blood
Starwoman's Sanctuary

Escaping Poison
Cyborg Security
Diaspora Worlds Bundle
Cyborg Liberation

Encanto Bay--Where Magic Happens
White Tiger Lover
The Psyvamp and the Professor
Holly Jolly Vampire
Single Mom, Vampire Lover

Far Stars Universe
Stranded on Grzbt
Christmas Cookies in Space
Pardblood, A Second Chance Romance

Love on the Space Frontier
Stars Between Us

Realms of Glister
Orc In Winter
Bridal Faire

Urloon
Refugees on Urloon

Standalone
Her Accidental Angel
Warm Winter Fantasies Collection